THE LEAVES CHANGE
in Autumn

ERMA JONES

Copyright © 2024 **Star Light Publishing**

All rights reserved. No part of this publication may be reproduced, distributed, or transmitted in any form or by any means, including photocopying, recording, or other electronic or mechanical methods, without the prior written permission of the publisher, except in the case of brief quotations embodied in critical reviews and certain other noncommercial uses permitted by copyright law. For permission requests, write to the publisher, addressed "Attention: Book Rights and Permission," at the address below.

Published in the United States of America

ISBN 978-1-960684-77-6 (SC)
ISBN 978-1-960684-75-2 (HC)
ISBN 978-1-960684-76-9 (Ebook)

Star Light Publishing
222 West 6th Street
Suite 400, San Pedro, CA, 90731
ermajones23@yahoo.com

Order Information and Rights Permission:

Quantity sales. Special discounts might be available on quantity purchases by corporations, associations, and others. For details, contact the publisher at the address above.

For Book Rights Adaptation and other Rights Permission. Call us at toll-free 1-888-945-8513 or send us an email at admin@stellarliterary.com.

Chapter 1

TAYLOR LET DOWN the sun visor to shield herself from the torrid sun that blazed overhead. She rolled up the window of her used 2014 Nissan Pathfinder and turned on the air-conditioning. The cool air hit her face and moved down her neck, resting on her chest. She began to relax as the air cooled off the inferno in her car.

She drove up to the corner of Main Street and First and stopped at the light. The traffic was light for the time of day, so Taylor was glad to go to the grocery store. She had to cook dinner for her father— something she had proudly done every night since her mother passed away.

She loved driving down Main Street. It looked like a town from the Wild West with its old Western brick buildings. The buildings were build close together, each displaying colorful signs with names emblazoned on each one. The diner had a yellow sign that read "Benny's Diner," And its large windows enabled passersby to see the customers sitting at the booths. The barber had the red, white, and blue barber's pole, and the bookstore had a light blue sign that read "Andy's Books." Taylor loved the library the most with its old white Roman columns. It was one of the oldest buildings on Main Street. The sheriff's office was the newest, built a couple of years earlier. It now housed up to fifty prisoners.

The light turned green, and Taylor stepped on the gas. She drove down Main Street, thinking about the day her mother passed away. She had been only fifteen, and her mother had been battling breast cancer.

Taylor could remember the nights her mother would come home from chemotherapy sick to her stomach, unable to eat dinner.

She remembered how she felt when her mother lost all her hair and how skinny she became. Her mother knew that she was going to lose her battle with breast cancer, so she tried to stay in good spirits. Taylor remembered the day of the funeral and how she felt when the whole town came out to support the family.

Taylor drove past the sheriff's office where her father worked. Her father, Sheriff Daniel Murphy, was proud of his job. He took it seriously, and for a town of 27,000, there were hardly any major crimes or murders. Not like the crime in the big cites. People felt safe in San Juan. You could raise your family there and not be scared to let your children play in the yard.

People gave that credit to Sheriff Murphy. Taylor and her father were the only two at home. For reasons that Taylor didn't understand, her father never got married again. He wouldn't even date. Taylor noticed that some of the single women in town were interested, but he would not pursue it.

He'd stopped going to church too. When Taylor's mother was alive, they wouldn't miss a Sunday. But now her father went to the office on Sunday, and Taylor had to go to church by herself. Taylor looked forward to the time she spent with her father. He would tell her stories about his childhood, like how he got the scar on his leg when diving into the river off an old wooden deck. He would tell her about the people he'd arrested that day or how he had to rescue Mrs. Scott's cat out of the tree.

Taylor thought that she would make a meatloaf and some roasted potatoes, but she discovered that she didn't have any potatoes. So she had to go to the store. She pulled into the parking lot, which was almost empty. She drove to the middle of the lot and parked. She was about to get out of her car when she saw a dark blue 2016 Mustang. Taylor's pulse pounded, and her palms began to sweat; waves moved through her stomach. It was Anton Guevara's car; he was in the store.

Taylor had had a crush on Anton for as long as she could remember. Anton was the handsomest man in San Juan County, and she had seen them all. She remembered how Anton would sit on the bleachers at the high school football stadium and talk to the girls. There were always two girls he would talk to: Tammy and Ashley. They were loose girls who wore tight clothes and too much makeup. They hardly ever went to class, and they hung out at Leo's almost every night. Leo's was the local bar on Wilson Drive where all the young people who were old enough to drink hung out.

All the girls wanted to date Anton, but he only went for the fast, loose girls. Taylor wished sometimes that she was one of those girls. Maybe Anton would notice her. But like all the other boys in this dumb town, he didn't have the nerve to talk to the girl who had a sheriff for a father. "Aren't no guys getting close to my daughter," the sheriff would say. Especially not a felon, and that's what Anton was. He was as bad as they got. It would do the sheriff good to lock him up and throw away the key.

Taylor got out of her car, pressed the door lock on her remote, and walked up the parking lot to the store. Jonathan Christensen came out of the store. He was cute, tall, and thin with a head full of blond hair and a pair of eyes that looked like the sky. He would be the ideal candidate for a boyfriend. He was smart—a premed student at the university—and his father owned the grocery store.

He walked over to a couple of carts in the lot and pushed them to the entrance. He looked up and saw Taylor, and something intense flared up inside of him. He could feel the weakness in his knees. He watched her walk up the lot, and he smiled. Taylor smiled back as she moved toward him.

"Hi," he said in a low, charming voice. Jonathan's voice would have sent shivers down Taylor's spine if she hadn't had such a crush on Anton. Anton was the guy she was interested in, not Jonathan, even though Jonathan would be her father's ideal pick. Jonathan came from a well-respected family in town and would one day be a leader in the community, but he didn't make Taylor's heart sing like the thought of Anton did.

"Hi," Taylor said with a smile, trying not to show too much interest. "Did you go to biology on Tuesday?" Jonathan asked. "I had a clinic appointment and was unable to make it."

"Yes, I did. We have a quiz on Thursday, and you have to be there since we are going over the notes for the midterm."

"Do you have the notes for Tuesday?" Jonathan asked. "Yes."

"Could I copy them?" "Sure."

"Thanks." Jonathan looked as if he were going to say something else, but instead he turned and began to push the carts through the doors. Taylor walked slowly behind him, grabbed a cart, and went into the grocery store.

The grocery store was chilly, hitting Taylor's arms like a cool breeze in winter. Taylor welcomed it because the ninety-degree heat outside was unbearable. She looked around and saw Susan at the register talking to Mrs. Johnson, and as usual, Mrs. Johnson had a lot of coupons.

The store isn't so busy, so my time here should be short, she thought. She went down the cereal aisle and found her father's favorite cereal: plain Cheerios. She then turned the corner and saw Mrs. Smith yelling at the new stock boy.

"I said I want light mayonnaise," Mrs. Smith snapped.

The stock boy rushed to find her product. Taylor hurried and turned down the canned goods aisle in hopes of avoiding Mrs. Smith. She picked up a can of tomato sauce and placed it in her cart.

"I'm looking for chickpeas." Mrs. Smith's voice rang out through the aisles. Taylor placed a few more cans in her cart and then headed for the produce section of the store. She turned out of the canned goods aisle and saw Mrs. Smith making a fuss about the bread. The stock boy who was helping her looked confused and upset.

Taylor walked over to produce where she saw Anton. Her heart skipped a beat, and she felt weak in the knees. She had to stop and catch her breath, so she just stood there and watched Anton as he was putting tomatoes in a basket that he was carrying. She watched how gently he picked up each tomato, carefully placing the tomatoes in the basket with his perfectly manicured fingers. Taylor loved the way Anton dressed; he wore a white T-shirt, a pair of straight-legged blue jeans, and a pair of black combat boots, which made him look devilish and terribly handsome.

He was a tall man with a medium build. He was built purely of muscle. There was no fat on him. She looked at his face as he looked down at the tomatoes, and her heart pounded double time when she studied his clear olive skin; his long, thin nose; his thick, neatly trimmed eyebrows; and his perfectly trimmed bread. His hair hung long, brushing the tops of his shoulders. To Taylor, he was the cutest guy in Texas. She walked over toward him, and he looked up at her with the prettiest eyes she had ever seen.

He smiled and gave her a little wave. Taylor's heart melted as she looked down at his basket.

"My mother is making a stew," he said, smiling at Taylor.

Shivers ran down Taylor's spine as she looked into Anton's soft brown eyes. She knew she shouldn't be talking to him. Anton wasn't the sort of person that good girls talked to. He had seen the inside of a jail more than a normal person, and it was rumored that he had killed a man or two. They say that he beat the two men with a baseball bat and left them bleeding to die, but they could never pin it on him. The sheriff said that Anton thought he was above the law and could do whatever the hell he wanted.

Anton looked at Taylor and couldn't help but notice how Taylor was looking at him. He knew that she had a crush on him but didn't know that it was so intense. He felt smug, and this intense feeling began to grow. Taylor looked around the store to take her gaze off Anton when she noticed her next-door neighbor Mrs. Smith approaching her.

Mrs. Smith was one of the older women in San Juan who was the keeper of the town gossip, and she seemed to know everything about everybody. She was a short, slender, dark-skinned black lady whose rich husband died and left her a fortune. Now she had nothing but time on her hands. When there were rumors flying around about someone, Mrs. Smith was in the center of it.

"Taylor, are you shopping for your daddy's supper?" Mrs. Smith asked, looking at Anton with displeasure and foul contemp.

"Yes, Mrs. Smith," Taylor answered, frightened by what the woman might be thinking.

"Then I trust you are going straight home to get started on it then," she said, frowning at Taylor. "Yes, Mrs. Smith."

Mrs. Smith took her cart and pushed it toward the frozen food aisle.

"What a basket case," Anton said, laughing.

"Yeah. A real nut job," Taylor added.

They both laughed until Mrs. Smith was out of sight.

"What are you doing tonight?" Anton asked, looking down at Taylor. "I have to cook dinner for my father, and then I'm going to study a little before I turn in."

"Oh, why don't you come down to Leo's tonight, just for little while?" Anton asked nicely. "I'm going to drop this off at my mother's and then head down there myself. I've never seen you there."

"I know," Taylor said. "I've been busy lately, and Leo's isn't really a place I care to hang out at."

What a bitch, Anton thought. He knew what type of girl Taylor was. She wasn't like those tramps who hung out at Leo's and he and his friends used up night after night. *Yep. The sheriff raised her right—like he is trying to clean up the town. Wouldn't it be a slap in the face if the sheriff knew I was using her up too? A real slap.*

"Come on … It will be fun," Anton pleaded with puppy dog eyes. Taylor looked at Anton's soft, round brown eyes and the warmth of his ruby-red lips, and her heart melted like butter.

"Okay. I'll be there around eight," she said with a smile. She then took her cart, turned, and headed for checkout.

Anton watched her as she went through checkout. He watched her dark brown hair flow down her back and examined her hourglass shape. She was the just the right type for him.

What make her want to talk to me? he wondered. *She has never giving the dudes in this town any play.*

Just then, Taylor looked in his direction, and he gave her a nice, warm wave as she walked out of the door.

Chapter 2

TAYLOR THREW HER groceries on the counter, took out her cell phone, and called Zoe, who had been her friend since the eighth grade. They had been through everything together.

When Taylor's mother died, Zoe and her mother helped Taylor and her aunt prepare the food for the repast. Zoe also helped Taylor get over the loss of her mother by taking her places and hanging out with her. Zoe knew how bad Taylor had a crush on Anton. She'd known since the tenth grade. Zoe felt that Anton was too wild for Taylor, and she warned Taylor of this many times. But Taylor still had her crush, so Zoe listened like a good friend would. The phone rang, and Zoe answered. "Hello?" "I did it," Taylor said excitedly. "Did what?" Zoe asked, laughing. "You know … I talked to Anton."

"You're crazy. What is your father going to say about this?" Zoe asked. "Who?"

"Your father … you know, the sheriff."

"I don't know. I have though that far ahead," Taylor admitted.

"You know Anton has been giving that man hell ever since his family moved to this town."

"I know, but Anton isn't really a bad person. He just needs a little guidance."

"And you are going to give it to him, huh?"

"He asked me to meet him a Leo's tonight," Taylor said.

"Leo's?! You know your father doesn't want you hanging around that place! If he finds out, he is going to kill you," Zoe said, becoming angry.

"That's why he is not going to find out," Taylor noted.

"How is he not going to find out, Taylor? Everybody in this town knows who goes in and out of Leo's. Someone will definitely tell him."

"I'm a big girl now. I can go wherever I want ... It's not like I'm still a teenager," Taylor protested, trying to convince herself more than Zoe.

"Okay, so that means you are going." Zoe gave in, not really knowing how to stop her friend from making a mistake.

"Yes. I have to find something to wear. I want to look sexy, but not too dressed up."

"Why don't you wear that dress you wore to you luncheon?" Zoe suggested. "It's nice, short, and fits your body well. It's the perfect outfit for a place like Leo's."

Taylor thought for a minute, and then a smile crept across her face. "You think so?"

"Trust me."

"Thank you, Zoe. You are a lifesaver." "You're welcome. I'll talk to you later."

"Goodbye," Taylor said as she pushed a button to end the call.

Taylor hurried to start dinner, running around the kitchen collecting pots and peeling potatoes. She wanted dinner to be perfect when her father came home, because she wanted him to be pleased when she told him about Anton.

Taylor's father always listened to her, and he had never objected to any of her decision in the past. After all, her father always tried to satisfy her. She thought that he would approach this situation with an open mind. Taylor finished dinner, ran to her room, and pulled out the dress Zoe was talking about. It was a thin beige dress that zipped up the side. She looked at it and spread it out on her bed.

She then went to her closet and pulled out her beige high heels and her beige clutch purse. Just then, Taylor heard the back door slam. It was her father, and from the sound of it, he was not in a good mood. Taylor entered the kitchen and began to put the food on the kitchen island.

"You wouldn't believe what kind of a day I had," he said, sitting down at the Island.

"What kind?" Taylor asked, looking at him.

He was a tall man with a medium build, coal-black hair, and a little gray in his beard. A lot of the women in town thought he was handsome, but to Taylor he was just daddy.

"Ethan attacked Mary Williams with a baseball bat today. He was angry that she had cut him off at the intersection near Green and Pine. This is the third time this week that we've gotten a call on Ethan.

"Yesterday he got into it with the store clerk at the pharmacy over the price of a bottle of shampoo. His temper is really getting the best of him."

"What are you going to do about it?" Taylor asked.

"Well, we arrested him and the prosecutor–you know Joe–is going to charge him with felony aggravated battery in a public place," Sheriff Murphy said, feeling sorry for Ethan, who had once been his friend. They had gone to school together and used to go fishing together until Pam, Ethan's wife of twenty years, had died. He hadn't been the same since.

Sheriff Murphy understood how he felt. On many occasions, he had wanted to crawl in a hole himself after Mary died, but he fought to keep the will to keep going day after day. He drug himself out of bed for Taylor's sake and the sake of the town. He had too much responsibility to fall apart. Besides, Mary wouldn't want that. He had to keep fighting for Taylor.

He tried to give Ethan some advice, but it fell on deaf ears. Ethan just kept to himself. He wouldn't talk to anyone and was very short tempered. People take grief differently. *Some people don't know how to let go*, the sheriff thought as he ate his dinner. The sheriff thought that he had done well. Taylor was happy. She hadn't wanted for anything since her had mother died, and his sister had been a big help with Taylor growing into the woman she had become—something he wouldn't have been able to do on his own.

The doorbell rang, and the sound echoed throughout the quiet house. The sheriff jumped at the sound, and his heart gave a little flutter.

"I'll get it," Taylor said as she ran out of the kitchen and into the living room.

As she opened the door, she was surprised to see it was Jonathan Taylor. She hadn't expected to see him so soon.

"I came over to get the notes, if you don't mind," he said with a smile.

The sheriff walked into the living room to see who was at the door.

"Who is it?" he asked.

"It's Jonathan," Taylor said as she motioned for Jonathan to come in. The sheriff smiled as Jonathan came in.

"Sit down," he said as he reached out to shake Jonathan's hand. "Thank you, sir," Jonathan said.

The sheriff liked Jonathan and thought he was a respectable boy. He was a good student, his parents were good friends with him, and Jonathan never gave them any problems. He went to the university and worked part time at his father's store. The sheriff saw how Jonathan liked Taylor and wouldn't mind if they went out. Taylor had never brought a boy home before. Maybe she was too shy to talk to boys, but she wasn't getting any younger.

I asked Mary out when I was eighteen, the sheriff thought. "I'll leave you two to talk," the sheriff said with a smile.

When Taylor looked at her father, she could tell how happy he was to see that Jonathan was over to talk to her. And yet, she still wasn't interested in Jonathan. She wanted to talk to Anton. She began to wonder and worry about how her father would react when he found out she was going to meet Anton later that night. She forced herself to put such thoughts out of her mind.

I'm an adult now, she thought. *I make my own decision.*

Jonathan looked at Taylor. He knew the sheriff was happy that he was over to talk to her. He wanted to talk to Taylor for a long time, but Taylor didn't seem to be interested. Maybe if she knew her father didn't mind she wouldn't feel so shy about it.

"I'll get my notebook," Taylor said as she walked in to the hall. Jonathan sat on the couch and pulled out his notebook and a pen.

Taylor came back and sat down next to him and noticed he had changed clothes from earlier that day and his cologne smelled extra good.

"Here are the notes," Taylor said as she flipped to the section containing the notes he needed.

Jonathan looked at Taylor's pearl-white skin and pink cheeks. He could feel the warmth of her breath on his cheeks moving up to his ear. A warm feeling grew over him, and he had the urge to kiss her on the lips. Taylor looked at him and handed him the notes. Jonathan smiled and took the notes. He looked over them and then began to write.

"Don't forget the quiz on Thursday," Taylor said.

"I'll be there. Anything else new happen at school on Tuesday?" Jonathon said, trying to make conversation.

"Not too much. Mr. Bookstien just showed us slides of reproducing cells. You didn't miss too much," Taylor noted. "Do you want me to get you anything? We were eating dinner."

Jonathan looked surprised. "You cooked?" he said, teasing. "Yes. I'm a good cook."

"Who taught you how to cook? "My mother, but mostly my aunt." "Really? You'll have to cook for me one day." "One day," Taylor said.

"I have some tickets to see OneRepublic in Austin. Would you like to go with me?" Jonathan asked.

"You got tickets?" Taylor said excitedly. "Everybody was trying to get their hands on a pair of those tickets."

"Yeah, well ... Do you want to go with me?"

Taylor wanted to go, but she had a date with Anton. "Can I let you know tomorrow?"

Jonathan was a little disappointed, but he smiled and said, "Sure ... tomorrow." He then packed his things in his bag and stood up. "I'll talk to you tomorrow then?"

"Yes, tomorrow," Taylor said smiling as she led Jonathan to the door. She closed the door and looked at her watch. It was six o'clock. She had to get ready for that night. She ran to her bathroom, turned on the shower, and began to get ready. She put on the beige dress she'd laid out on her bed. She carefully applied her makeup, looked in the full-sized mirror on her bedroom door, and arranged her clothes, trying to become the type of girl she thought Anton would want. When she was through, she got her purse and her car keys and headed for the door.

Her father was sitting in his recliner in the living room watching television. He turned and looked at Taylor as she was walking out the door.

"Where are you going?" he asked, surprised.

"I'm going out for a little while to hang with my friends, Dad. I'll be back. Don't wait up," she said as she hurried out.

Taylor got into her car and began her drive down Main Street. It was dark—a kind of thick dark you could cut with a knife. The only light was the dim yellow light from the light pole just up beyond the post office. It felt strange going to Leo's. She and Zoe had made a promise to each other to never go there, because they didn't want to be in the same category with Tammy and Ashley, the town whores. But Anton hung out there, and Taylor had wanted to hook up with Anton for a long time.

Taylor remembered how Anton would ride around town on his motorcycle. He liked fast things like that because he thought that made him cool. It made him stand out among his friends, and all the girls liked him even more. Every day he would have a different girl on the back of his motorcycle riding through the town.

Taylor could hear the motor as it sped through the streets. Everyone knew it was Anton. On many occasions, she dreamed of riding on back of his motorcycle, the two of them speeding down the highway with the wind at their backs. They would leave this dusty town behind with no cares in the world—just her and Anton.

Then she thought of how mean he could be. Once he got into it with this guy name Sid. Anton beat him up badly and then threaten his whole family. Sid's parents moved after that incident, because they didn't trust that the sheriff could protect them. Anton and his gang had a bed reputation, and all the older people in town were afraid to stand up to him—but not the sheriff. Sheriff Murphy wasn't afraid of any of the boys in town, and he did a good job keeping them in order.

A few years ago, Anton robbed a liquor store. He held a gun to the store clerk's head and demanded money. Sheriff Murphy arrested him, and Anton served three years in the county jail. Mike, Anton's buddy, was no angel either. While Anton was in jail, Mike beat up Amy, his girlfriend, breaking her arm and putting her in the hospital. Another friend named Frank claimed he tried to stop him, but the sheriff didn't believe him. Amy wouldn't press charges on Mike, so he walked away. She ended up leaving town.

Taylor had never seen Anton with just one women. He hung out with the girls at Leo's. They were fast and wide and pretty, and if that's the kind of girl Anton liked, that's how she was going to be. Once Taylor was coming out of the pharmacy when she saw Anton getting on his bike.

"You want a ride?" he asked. "No," she answered.

He had just gotten out of jail, and she was afraid of what her father might think. Instead, she just watched Anton ride away. He didn't ride his motorcycle much anymore. He was in to fast cars like his Mustang.

The parking lot at Leo's was crowed for a Thursday night. Taylor had to circle around two times before she could find a spot. The lights were extra bright on the light poles in the middle of the lot. The ground was newly paved, and the freshly painted white lines reflected the light. Taylor turned off her engine and got out of the car. She could hear the music blaring from the square two-story building just ahead of her. When she reached the door, she could smell the mixture of beer and cigarettes in the air. People were standing along the wall near the entrance showing signs of drunkenness.

Inside Leo's, it was dark, and all the stools were taken at the long bar in the rear of the place. There were young people sitting at tables in the middle of the floor. Some were sitting at booths along the wall. People filled the dance floor in the back corner, and others were shooting pool. The music was loud, and the crowd was filled with people talking and laughing, trying to hear themselves over the music.

When Taylor walked in, it seemed as if the whole place stopped and stared. She looked around and saw Anton by a pool table in the back. He was with his usual gang, Frank and Mike. Mike was a mean son of a bitch. He'd had his own run-ins with the law and was known for beating his women. Frank was a coward and did whatever the hell Anton or Mike told him to do, but he wouldn't fight on his own. "Taylor!" Anton called, waving to her from the back.

"Taylor? Taylor murphy?" Frank questioned. "You must be out of your mind."

"You know the sheriff isn't going to like this," Mike protested. "With what we are in to, we don't need the law breathing down our necks."

"Don't worry about it," Anton reassured them. "It won't get out of control."

Mike looked at Anton. "We'll see."

Taylor made her way to the back and could feel the eyes of the other girls watching her as she approached Anton. She felt a little intimidated. "Hey, Anton," she said as she walked up to him.

He leaned over and kissed her on the cheek. "You know Frank and Mike," he said with a smile.

"Yes, I do. Hello," Taylor said with a smile.

"Whatever," Mike said as he leaned over to shoot pool. "Hey," Frank said as he reached out to shake her hand.

"Let's sit over here," Anton said, pointing to an empty table and flashing a smile. "Do you want something to drink?" "I'll take a beer," Taylor said, returning a smile.

He motioned to the bar, holding up two fingers. "Two beers," he said loudly, getting the bartenders attention.

Tom, one of the deputy sheriffs, was sitting at the bar watching Taylor as she talked to Anton. "Tell me how many beers she has," he told the bartender.

"Will do," the bartender said as he took Anton his beers.

Tom pulled out his cell phone and dialed Sheriff Murphy. The sheriff's phone went straight to voice mail, so Tom just sat there and slowly sipped his beer.

Taylor looked around the bar and noticed that people were watching her talk to Anton. She didn't know whether to feel intimidated or proud. "So, you go to Texas State University?" Anton asked, trying to get her attention.

"Yes," Taylor answered. "I'm a senior and graduate in May. Then I'm going back to Europe for the summer."

"You went to Europe?" Anton asked. "Tell me about that."

"Yeah, it was great. I've been to England, where I saw Big Ben and Buckingham Palace. I saw a real bull fight in Spain, and I visited Vatican City in Italy. I especially liked Italy. The food was great."

"I've never been anywhere. I don't think I've ever been out of Texas," Anton said sadly.

"Well you should take the time to go one day. It's a whole, big world outside Texas."

Anton looked away as Taylor was talking. *She's been everywhere. What the hell is she doing here talking to me?* he thought to himself. He looked back at Taylor, who was looking at him like he was the prince of England. He smiled. *Just go with it*, he thought.

Deputy Tom continued to watch Taylor as she drank her beer.

"What in the hell is she doing here?" he asked the bartender.

The bartender shrugged his shoulders in wonder.

"Taylor is too nice of a girl to get mixed up with that scum Anton Guevara," the deputy continued in disgust.

"Do you want another beer?" Anton asked Taylor.

Taylor looked at her empty glass. She didn't really like beer, but she was afraid that Anton would think that she was too nice or stuck up to drink with him. So she nodded her head yes.

Anton motioned to the bar. "Two beers." he yelled.

Taylor looked at Anton, and her heart skipped a beat. She noticed how he ordered the drinks with authority and a coolness that she had never witnessed in the boys in her class at school. She had waited her whole life for this moment, and now it was finally here. One day when she was a teenager, she had been visiting her father at the sheriff's station when she saw Anton for the first time. He was being arrested for fighting and disturbing the peace. Her father had set him in a chair near the desk where she was sitting. He was still angry and lashing out at her father, who told him that he was going to add resisting arrest to his many charges.

Taylor looked at him and couldn't understand why such a handsome guy who could have everything could be so bed.

"Do you want to dance?" Anton asked, pointing to the dance floor. "Sure," Taylor said, excited.

He took her by the hand and led her to the dance floor. Taylor could feel the people looking as he pulled her into his arms. The music was loud as they swayed back and forth. Her heart was pounding, and her palms were sweating as Anton pulled her close to him. She could hear his heartbeat, and his breath felt warm on her cheeks. She closed her eyes and imagined they were dancing in a grand ballroom in Buckingham Palace. Anton was the prince, and she was the princess, and there was no town and no Sheriff Murphy. For a brief moment, they were the only ones in the room. Moving to the music as one, Taylor lay her head on Anton's chest and closed her eyes.

He pulled her close to him and squeezed her tight. She felt warm and safe. She didn't want the music to end. She could have held on to Anton all night. But the music stopped, and Anton led her back to the table.

Deputy Tom watched in amazement and anger as Anton and Taylor danced.

"The sheriff is going to have a hard time believing this," he said as he drank the rest of his beer. He watched Taylor walk back to her chair and then checked the time. It was twelve thirty.

"Do you want another beer?" Anton asked in a voice that sounded far away. Taylor was still thinking about the dance.

"Taylor? Taylor!" Anton called loudly

"Huh? What you say?" she asked. "Do you want another beer?"

I better get home. If I take another beer, who knows what might happen, Taylor thought to herself. "No, I better get home," she said to Anton.

Anton looked disappointed as she gathered her things. "I'll walk you to the door," he said.

Deputy Tom grabbed his hat and walked slowly behind them. They walked out of the bar and slowly headed toward Taylor's car.

"Will I see you tomorrow?" Anton asked hopefully. "Yes. I had a good time," Taylor said with a smile.

Anton leaned over and kissed her on the lips. Taylor's knees buckled, and her heart began to pound as she turned and opened the car door. "See you tomorrow, and drive safely," Anton said as he began to back up. "I will," Taylor said as she pulled away.

Deputy Tom got into his car and slowly drove past Anton as he walked slowly back inside Leo's.

Chapter 3

THE DINER WAS crowed for a Friday afternoon. Jack had only two waitresses working that day: Alice and Maria. They were busy working on the register and waiting on tables. The customers were hungry and anxious to be waited on. Sheriff Murphy and Deputy Jerry walked into the diner and waited to be seated. The sun was high, and the temperature was in the nineties. Beads of sweat ran down the sheriff's face, and his mouth was dry. His tongue felt thick and rough like sandpaper. The cool air conditioner was a help, but the sheriff wasn't going to be comfortable until he had a cool glass of Coke.

"I'll be with you in a second," Alice said as she took a couple at the booth their food.

"Sheriff!" Deputy Tom called. "Over here!" He waved for the sheriff and Deputy Jerry to come and sit with him at a booth in the rear.

Sheriff Murphy walked slowly toward the deputy when he noticed Tammy and Ashley looking at him and whispering to each other. "Hey, Tom," the sheriff said as he sat down.

Jerry sat down beside him, and Alice brought them two menus. "It's hot today," the sheriff said as he took off his hat.

"I know, but there isn't much going on today—just the same old thing. Mrs. Scott called because she couldn't find her cat. He didn't come home last night," Tom said.

"I think Mrs. Scott just wants some attention. She is all alone in that big house, and she doesn't have anyone to talk to. She calls 911 and tries to hold a conversation with Gloria," the sheriff said.

"I was talking to the mayor. We need activities for our older citizens in the community. There is a lot for our young people to do, but there isn't much for the older ones. They feel neglected," Tom noted. He looked at the sheriff as he was talking. *Speaking of activities* ... he thought to himself. He thought about the best way to tell the sheriff about Taylor and Anton.

Tammy and Ashley giggled loudly from another booth, and Sheriff Murphy looked in their direction.

"You ready to order, Sheriff?" Alice said, ready to write down their order. "I'll have the pancake special," Deputy Jerry said.

"You can give me a double cheeseburger and some fries," the sheriff said. "Would you like anything to drink with that?" Alice asked.

"I'll have a Coke" said the sheriff.

"I'll have a tall, cold glass of milk," Deputy Jerry said. Alice walked over to the counter to put in their order.

Sheriff Murphy notice that Tammy and Ashley were looking at him and giggling.

Tom looked over at them. "Sheriff, do you know that Taylor went out last night?" he asked, feeling a little uneasy.

The sheriff's eyes widened as he looked at Tom. He then looked back at Tammy and Ashley. "I know she told me she was going to the movies with Zoe and some friends from school."

Tom's heart sunk. His tongue felt thick, and he hated himself for what he was about to say. "No, sir. She was at Leo's last night." "What Leo's?" Deputy Jerry asked, surprised.

Sheriff Murphy didn't say anything. He just waited for Tom to finish. "Yes," Tom said as he looked from Jerry to Murphy.

"She was having drinks with Anton Guevara. She had a couple of drinks, and they danced."

"They danced?" Jerry said as he looked wide-eyed at the sheriff. Sheriff Murphy was surprised that Taylor would disobey him and go to a place like Leo's. A knot formed in his stomach, and he tried not to show his anger. Ashley looked in the direction of the sheriff and let out a loud giggle.

"Were Tammy and Ashley there last night?" Jerry asked.

"They're there all the time," Tom said as he looked in their direction.

Alice came with their orders, and Sheriff Murphy's stomach did flip-flops as he looked down at his plate.

"Where is Taylor now, if you don't mind me asking?" Jerry said as he looked at the sheriff.

Sheriff Murphy picked up his burger and forced a bite. Then he put it down and said, "She better be in class."

"What time does she gets home?" Tom asked.

"Around three." Sheriff Murphy looked at Tammy and Ashley, and his anger began to rise. His face turned red, and his heart began to pound. He felt as though he had been running. *Out of all the boys in this town, why Anton?* he thought. *That no-good son of a bitch is not going to get his hands on my daughter. I'll kill him. I'll burn his mother's house down.*

Deputy Jerry saw the expression on the sheriff's face. "Don't go jumping to conclusions, Sheriff," he said, as he thought the sheriff was going to have a fit. "She was just talking to the boy."

"It looks like a little more than just talking," Tom said.

"Shut up, Tom," Jerry said. "Anton isn't all that bad. He has a job now, and he hasn't really been in any trouble since he got out of jail."

"Anton is a no-good, troublemaking hoodlum," Tom said loudly.

Everyone in the diner looked in their direction, and Tammy and Ashley stopped laughing.

"Keep your voice down," Jerry said.

"Taylor is too good of a person to get caught up in Anton's mess," Tom said

"All I'm saying is they were just talking. We don't know anything yet. Just don't jump to any conclusions, Sheriff."

The sheriff looked at Jerry and Tom and forced down the last of his cheeseburger.

"How would you feel if it was your daughter at Leo's with Anton, Frank, and Mike? You would shoot them," Tom said.

"No, I would not," Jerry insisted.

"Yes you would. I know I would. I wouldn't give Anton the chance to ruin my daughter and then go on with another notch in his belt," Tom said.

The sheriff motioned for the check. He looked in Tammy and Ashley's direction. He knew they were having a laugh about Taylor at his expense.

But as much as they laughed and cracked jokes, Taylor would never be as low as them.

"Tom, I'll talk to you later," the sheriff said as he stood up and walked to the register to pay his check. Then he and Deputy Jerry walked out of the door. The sheriff got in his car. Deputy Jerry looked at him and could see the anger and hurt in his friend's eyes.

"Daniel, don't go jumping to conclusions. You know your daughter. Taylor wouldn't do anything stupid."

"Taylor is a good girl. She always sees the good in people. She's not experienced in these things. She's a dreamer, and when she puts her mind on a project or problem, she tries to fix it. She doesn't know the danger of going out with a guy like Anton. I have to talk to her and straighten her out," the sheriff said.

"Don't yell at her or embarrass her. Treat her like a young adult and express your concerns. If you try to force her, you'll push her away," Deputy Jerry warned him.

"Taylor is a good girl. She has never disobeyed me before. I don't think she would disobey me now. I can talk to her. She will listen to me. Jonathan Christensen came over the other day, and I though they hit it off well. If

I tell her to go with Jonathan, she will listen."

Chapter 4

ANTON WALKED INTO his large one-bedroom apartment on the west side of town. He had been living here for three years now. He loved his apartment, because it was the first one he'd had since moving out of his mother's house. He looked around the comfortable open floor plan. He kept everything up nicely. His black leather couch sat in the middle of the living room with a large black ottoman in front of it. A matching black chair sat on the opposite side of the couch with a glass end table next to it. He had an entertainment center on the right wall that housed a sixty-inch high-definition television.

Anton walked into the kitchen and threw his mail on the counter. He then walked to the ottoman, picked up his remote, and turned on the television. He flipped through the channels before settling on the Syfy channel. There was a *Face Off* marathon on, one of his favorite shows.

He walked over to a large glass tank sitting on the left wall that housed a large green chameleon. The tank was filed with wood chips and tree branches that the lizard could climb on. He got an old coffee can from his refrigerator, reached in, and pulled out four superworms to feed to the lizard.

"Here, Charlie," he said as the chameleon swallowed down the worms. "You hungry, boy?" he asked as he looked through the glass tank at his pet.

He then went to the bathroom and washed his hands. He thought about the mail on the kitchen counter and walked to the kitchen to read it. He looked at a light bill and threw it on the counter. "Bill," he said.

He then looked at an advertisement and threw it on the counter.

"Junk," he said.

His heart jumped and traveled to his throat. It was a long white envelope addressed to him from Leavenworth US Army post in Kansas.

It was a letter from his father, who had been court-martialed and put in prison. Anton had been only fifteen years old when his father was sent to prison for killing a fellow soldier in the barracks at Fort Sam Houston where he was stationed. Anton's father had lost all his benefits and was now serving a life sentence.

That forced Anton's mom to move in with relatives in San Juan. She got a job as a housekeeper at the local hospital. Anton was so angry with his father that he lashed out and started to get in trouble himself. Jose Guevara, his mother's brother, said that Anton was going to end up like his father serving a life sentence. Anton's mother tried to help her son the best she could, and even when he lashed out at her, she never gave up on him or turned her back on him.

Anton's hand shook as he looked at the envelope. He set it on the counter and walked into the living room. Tears formed in his eyes, and he wiped at the tears as anger built up in his chest.

"How dare he write me after all these years. When I tried to contact him two years ago, he wouldn't see me. I don't need him now. I make my own way and have been doing so for nine years now," he said as he walked over to the window and looked out toward the street. The neighborhood was quiet, and the sun was just beginning to go down. The clouds looked orange and pink, and a yellow tent was in the blue sky. The crickets were chirping, but Anton got distracted by Mr. Moore's car engine on the street below. He was starting up his car and driving off.

Anton thought about the letter again, and it angered him, because he was curious to know what it said. He stormed across the room and snatched the letter off the counter.

"He was to evil to give me his name. I don't know how Mom stayed with him for all of those years," he said, feeling sick to his stomach. He tore open the envelope, and a feeling of hurt and isolation came over him as he unfolded the piece of notebook paper inside. A lump grew in his throat as he read the words.

> Dear, Son,
>
> I hope this letter find you well. I know you haven't heard from me since I've been in this hell hole, but I couldn't find the words to express what I'm really feeling. Your mother told me that you had has some run-in with the law down there in San Juan. I know that your rebellion and lashing out at your mother is a result of my absence. I know you blame me for not being there for you when you really needed me the most.

Tears began to fall down Anton's face, and he strained to see the letter. He wiped at his eyes and continued to read.

> Son, I just want you to know that I am sorry. I have become a born-again Christian, and I have learned to own up to my mistakes and accept responsibility. I know that the Lord has forgiven me, and in return, I have forgiven myself. I know the reason I am in prison is because of my own doing. I'm to blame—no one else. I hope that you can forgive me and that one day you can accept the Lord in your life and come to accept your mistakes so you can learn to forgive yourself and live a life free of guilt and blame. I'd like to share a verse with you. When I read it, I think of you. Proverbs 28: 13–14. I love you, Son. Take care.

Anton wiped the tears from his eyes as he folded the letter and stuck it back in the envelope. He walked over to the coat closet and put it on the shelf. His cell phone rang, and he walked over to ottoman and picked up his phone. It was Taylor. Mischief came over him, and he let it go to voice mail. He was amused at how easy he thought Taylor seemed to be. He knew she liked him, but he didn't know how much until after last night at Leo's. "I can take this as far as I want," he said as he laughed to himself. "I'll have her jumping through hoops. What will Murphy say about that? It's not like she's underage. She came to me in the store. She is asking for it."

Anton ran his hand through his hair as he walked over to lie down on the couch. The phone rang again. It was Taylor, and he grinned as he let it go to voice mail.

He thought of a football game. "Yep. I'm in the in zone," he said, pleased at the game he was playing on Taylor. "She doesn't know who I am, but she is going to find out. I wonder how fast I can get to home base." He looked over at the box of condoms on the kitchen counter. "Yep. This is going to be fun. And then I drop her like a hot potato. There won't be a thing the sheriff can do about it."

The doorbell rang, and Anton jumped up and peeked through the peep hole. It was Frank and Mike.

"Hey, guys," Anton said as he let them in.

Mike sat on the couch, and Frank sat on a stool at the kitchen counter. Anton sat down in the leather chair. The phone rang again, and he checked it and let it go to voice mail.

"Who was that?" Frank asked. Anton laughed. "Taylor." "Why didn't you answer it?" Frank asked.

"I'm conditioning her. I'm making her wait. If I'm available every time she calls, she won't be ripe enough when I want her to be."

"You can't play those kinds of games on that girl," Mike said. "If you are not interested, don't fuck with her. Besides, she really is a nice girl."

"And she likes you," Frank said.

"That's the idea. I want her to like me," Anton said, grinning.

"Leave that girl alone if you are not serious about her. You are going to make the sheriff angry, and he is going to come down hard on you," Mike said.

"What could he do?" Anton asked. "Taylor is a grown woman. I'm just having a little fun. No harm, no foul."

"The harm is you are going to be a dead duck," Frank said.

"Taylor is a good person, but I hate that son of a bitch sheriff. He thinks he is God, like he is perfect or something the way he looks down on certain people in this town. He thinks Taylor is perfect too. Well, I'm going to show that son of a bitch that Taylor ain't no better than us—Taylor, Zoe, none of those fuckers on the east end."

"You have a problem, Anton. You really need to get over yourself. You are going to hurt Taylor just to get back at the sheriff, and that's wrong," Mike said. "She hasn't done anything to you." "Yeah, you are just asking for trouble," Frank said.

"Trouble is my middle name," Anton said as he grinned at Frank.

Chapter 5

JONATHAN WAS WAITING for a computer in the school library. The library was full of students who were cramming for midterms.

A computer was finally available, so Jonathan immediately sat down because he only had one hour to use it. He was glad to be doing something, because he'd had Taylor on his mind all day. He had rehearsed the words he was going to say to her when he asked her to go study with him.

He was really surprised himself when he began to like Taylor. They'd been going to school together since the first grade, and he had never really had any interest in her until recently. Throughout high school he had gone steady with Sherry, a local girl he thought he would marry. But she broke it off with him when she was accepted at the University of Massachusetts. She told him that she didn't want a long-distance relationship. It had been four years, and they hardly even spoke anymore.

Jonathan's parents and the sheriff were good friends. The sheriff and Taylor had dinner over at Jonathan's house on many occasion. Taylor and Jonathan had become close friends, and Jonathan was beginning to have feeling for her.

During their four years of college, Taylor had grown to be a beautiful young woman. It seemed that it had happened right before Jonathan's eyes. He typed "DNA damage" in the computer and began printing out the information. His mother was very fond of Taylor and thought she was a very nice girl. She talked about her more than she did Sherry.

Jonathan thought that was important. He knew the sheriff was fond of him. He had sensed it while he was at the house on Wednesday. He knew it wouldn't be a problem if he and Taylor dated. *Maybe she's the one*, he thought, turning the possibility over in his head. It felt good to him. It felt right. The thought of Taylor made him happy.

His hour on the computer was over. He had just finished looking up his assignment online when a tall, skinny kid dropped his books down, waiting to use the computer. Jonathan got up and walked over to a row of tables where he saw Alex, his friend since high school. He was typing on his laptop. Alex had lived in San Juan almost as long as Jonathan and his father, who was Deputy Jerry—also good friends with the sheriff and Taylor.

Jonathan walked over to Alex and sat down quietly. Alex looked up and gave a quick nod. Jonathan looked over to the librarian's desk and saw Mrs. Lopez, who was very meticulous and kept to the library's bylaws. That meant quiet—no talking.

"You brought your laptop?" Jonathan asked.

"Oh, yeah. Where is yours?" Alex asked, surprised that Jonathan didn't have his.

"I left it at home. I get tired of carrying that thing around." "Dude ... You have a car!"

"I know. I'm tired. I can't wait until school is out," Jonathan said

"Dude, it starts all over again next year."

"I know," Jonathan said. "It seems like I've been going to school all of my life."

"You have," Alex pointed out. "I'm doing it," Jonathan said "Doing what?" asked Alex.

"I'm going to ask Taylor to go study whit me."

Alex looked at Jonathan and could tell he was nervous. "Man, just ask her. Don't think about it. Just do it. If you think about it, you are going to chicken out. She's just a girl—a very hot girl, but she bleeds just like you and me. The worse she can say is no.

"But she is not going to say no. I see how she looks at you in class.

You better hurry up before someone else does it.

"I don't want to get shot down. Taylor isn't like most girls. She is special. I want the moment to be right," Jonathan said

"Dude, you're not asking her to marry you. You are just asking her to go out with you," Alex said loudly.

Mrs. Lopez looked over at the table, and Jonathan scooted down in his seat.

"You are going to get us kicked out of here," Alex said

"That was you," Jonathan said, laughing. "I'll do it. I'll ask her tomorrow. I'm going to march over to her house, sit her down, and asked her."

Mrs. Lopez stepped out from behind her desk and walked up to Jonathan. She leaned down before speaking to him. "Young man, this is a library, not a park bench. If you want to talk, you have the freedom to do so outside. So please keep it down. This is a warning. The next time I'm going to asked you to leave." "Yes, Mrs. Lopez," Jonathan said.

Mrs. Lopez walked back to the desk and began checking out books. "This is a library, not a park bench," Alex said, mocking Mrs. Lopez. Jonathan laugh out loud.

Mrs. Lopez ran from behind the desk. "Get out! You two get out now!" she screamed.

Jonathan got up, laughing out loud. He gathered his books, and he and Alex walked out.

Chapter 6

TAYLOR WAS THROUGH preparing dinner. She turned on the television and watched the news. It had been another hot day, and she was glad to be in the air-conditioning. Her father wasn't going to be home for the next two hours, so she took the opportunity to take a long, cool bath. Taylor enjoyed the time she spent alone in the house when her father worked late. It was like having her own place. She couldn't afford her own place yet. She only had a part-time job and was a full-time student. It was important that she finish school. Her mother had wanted her to be a nurse ever since she was a little girl.

Her mother did not live to see her finish high school. Taylor's aunt took the role of mother. She had a cool job that allow her to travel, and she sometimes took Taylor with her. She never married and didn't have any children of her own, so Taylor was like a surrogate daughter. Sometimes she would spend more time with her aunt than her father.

Taylor finished her bath and went to her closet to find something sexy to wear. She had nice clothes, but they weren't sexy—not the type of clothes Tammy and Ashley wore. She thought Tammy and Ashley were so worldly and looked down on them, but she had seen how the boys reacted to them, which made her jealous. Taylor was cute—teddy bear cute—but she wasn't sexy. The boys didn't pull at her the way they did Tammy and Ashley, and she knew it was partly because her father was the sheriff and partly because she didn't hang around them enough.

Whatever the reason, things were going to change. She wasn't going to be like her aunt, pushing fifty and still single. Taylor wanted to have it all—a career and a man or two, starting with Anton.

The doorbell rang, and Taylor put on her robe and went to the door. She looked out and saw it was Jonathan. She opened the door and invited him in.

"I didn't see you at school today," he said.

"I was in a hurry. I didn't hang around," Taylor said.

"Oh, I'm sorry. Are you busy? I can come back," Jonathan said, looking at her robe.

"I was just having a bath. It was hot today, and I was just trying to cool off."

"Do you have a minute? I would like to talk to you," Jonathan said seriously.

"Well, Jonathan, my father will be home in a few minutes, and I have a lot of homework."

"Maybe tomorrow then," Jonathan said.

"Yeah, I promise I'll talk with you tomorrow."

"Okay," Jonathan said as he leaned over and kissed her on the cheek. Then he walked out, and Taylor closed the door. She ran to her room and pulled out her ripped jeans and white tank top, hurrying to get dressed. She didn't know why she liked Anton. To her, he was the handsomest dude in town. She knew he liked her too from the way she caught him looking at her at the diner when he was with his boys and at the supermarket the other day. She knew he wanted to talk to her but was scared of her father. That's why she gave him the opportunity.

Taylor was in the bathroom applying her makeup when her father came in. He went straight to the kitchen.

"Dinner is ready, Daddy," Taylor said, putting the dinner on the island. Sheriff Murphy looked at Taylor and noticed she was dressed to go out.

"Are you going somewhere tonight?" he asked as he began to eat.

"They are having a dance at school tonight," she said. "I thought I might go."

"Oh, is Jonathan going to be there?"

"I suppose so. All the kids who attended TSU are going to be there."

"I see."

"I talked to Tom today," the sheriff said as he looked at Taylor. "He told me you were at Leo's last night."

Taylor's eyes widened, and her heart began to pound. "Daddy, I can explain." "Explain."

"I met Anton the other day at the supermarket, and he asked me out. It was innocent. We only danced," she said. "He is not such a bad person once you get to know him. I really like him, Daddy."

Sheriff Murphy jumped in surprise. And his anger began to rise as he realized Taylor was really infatuated with Anton. "Taylor, Anton is a criminal. He just got out of jail."

"He is trying to get his life together. He doesn't do those things anymore," Taylor said as she began to cry.

"Anton is a punk hoodlum. He doesn't mean you any good. Get that nonsense out of your head. You can do better than Anton," the sheriff said. "You didn't give him a chance. You don't know how Anton could be."

"I know him well enough. I've known him for nine years, and he has given me nothing but trouble. You can do better than Anton," the sheriff said calmly. He then finished his meal, stood up, and went into the living room.

Taylor put the dishes in the dishwasher, and then an anger came over her. She stormed into the living room. "Anton isn't a bad person once you get to know him," she screamed.

Her father looked surprised at the response coming from Taylor. "Anton is a thug—a punk thug," he yelled back at the top of his voice. "He's a troublemaker and a bully, and I do believe he killed those men. If he didn't, he had something to do with it. Frank and Mike and that whole bunch are the worst punks to come along. Anton didn't even finish high school. His poor mother tried to make him go to school, but he would hang out at Leo's instead. And that Mike … the way he beat up on Amy. That's all they are good for. No, you stay the hell away from them." "Anton would never hit me," Taylor cried.

"You don't know that. I'm telling you for your own good. I know you don't see it right now, but you are going to make the biggest mistake of your life. That's why I'm here, Taylor—to keep you from messing up. You are not going to see that boy anymore," her father insisted.

"I'm a grown woman. My mistakes are for me to make, and me alone." Sheriff Murphy's heart dropped. Taylor's words were sharp, like a double-edged sword.

"You can't tell me who I can see or who I can't see." She took her keys off the coffee table and stormed out the door.

Sheriff Murphy walked over to his desk, picked up the phone, and called the office. "Gloria, is Tom still there?" he asked.

"No, Sheriff," the voice on the other end said. "He stepped out for a minute, but he should be back shortly."

"When he gets in, tell him to stop by my house on his way home."

"Will do, Sheriff."

Chapter 7

SHERIFF MURPHY WENT over to his rifle cabinet on the far wall in the living room, opposite the fireplace. He opened the door and pulled out his Smith and Wesson, cocked it, and looked through the barrel.

"I'll teach that son of a bitch," he said out loud as he reached for a box of shells. He walked over to the window and looked out into the dark, lonely street and at the empty space where Taylor's car once stood. "He thinks he's going to ruin my daughter. He's got another thing coming. I'll kill him first. I'll kill Taylor. She is not going to do me like this. Not now, not ever."

He walked over to his armchair, sat down, and began loading his rifle. He checked the time. It was 7:30. Deputy Tom had been off duty for and half an hour now. He'd called Gloria and told her to tell him to drop by on his way home. It seemed like eternity since Taylor had stormed out of the house. It killed him to think about what she might be doing at that moment.

He checked his watch again. It was 7:35. Every minute he waited on Tom seemed like a lifetime. Every second was more painful than the last. The doorbell rang, and Sheriff Murphy jumped up.

"Finally," he said as he rushed to the door. And to his surprise, Deputy Jerry was with Tom.

"Sheriff," Deputy Jerry said as he walked through the door. "Sheriff," Deputy Tom repeated.

Deputy Jerry walked into the living room and noticed the rifle leaning against the wall.

"Gloria told me that you wanted me to come by," Tom said as he noticed the rifle.

"Taylor ... Taylor," the sheriff said, trying to get the words out.

"Taylor? What about Taylor?" Jerry said.

"She's with that son of a bitch Anton," the sheriff said.

"I thought that you were going to talk to her," Jerry said.

"I did ... I tried. But she stormed out of here and said she was old enough to make her own decisions. Now she's out there doing God knows what with that boy."

"What do you want to do about it, Sheriff?" Tom said, putting his hand on his gun.

"Let's go find that son of a bitch and give him a test of this billy club," the sheriff said.

"I've been waiting on this for a long time," Tom said. "Let's put him in the hospital."

"Wait a minute, fellows," Jerry said, holding up his hands. "Let's not resort to violence. I mean, it could be innocent. She's just talking to the boy." "Just talking? Anton doesn't seem like the kind who just talks. He's taken advantage of her, and before you know it, she will be strung out on drugs and alcohol."

"Let's not jump to conclusions, Sheriff. Don't do something you're going to regret later," Jerry pleaded.

"Anton really got himself together after he got out of jail. He's got a job, and he helps his mother. Besides, you're not supposed to keep condemning a man for his past. The Bible teaches us not to condemn a man by judging him, or we'll be judged by the same measure."

The sheriff looked at Deputy Jerry and threw his hands up.

"This is not the time for a Bible lesson, Jerry. My little girl is out there with that son of a bitch doing God knows what, and I bet you Anton ain't thinking about the Bible."

"What I'm trying to say is this isn't the way to go about this." "What do you suggest then, Jerry?"

"Talk to Taylor. See where her head is at. Express your concerns and talk to her like she is an adult. In the meantime, I'll talk to Anton."

"I say our way is better. Anton only understands one way," said Tom.

"Tom."

"What, Jerry?"

"Sheriff, give it a few days before you confront Anton," Jerry said. The sheriff looked at Jerry and then walked over to the window. "I'll give you a few days, but if this doesn't end, I'm going to end it my way." "I'll talk to Anton and see where his head is at. Just give me a few days." Sheriff Murphy picked up his rifle and returned it to the rifle cabinet. He then looked at Jerry. "I wanted to shoot Anton. You are his guardian angel. I'm going to give it a few days like you asked, but something's got to give."

"I'll pray on it," Jerry said.

Tom looked at the sheriff. "Well, that's that then," he said.

"I've got to get home. Helen cooked a meat loaf," Jerry said as he walked over to the door.

"That sounds good," the sheriff said.

"I've got to run too. I've got to feed my dog, Buddy," Tom said Jerry open the door and began walking down the driveway. "Tom," the sheriff said in a low voice. "I'll call you."

Tom looked at Jerry and then looked at the sheriff. "I'm looking forward to it."

Chapter 8

TAYLOR DROVE OVER to the diner where Zoe worked. She went in and sat at the counter. Zoe was waiting on tables in the back. Taylor picked up a menu as if she was going to order as Zoe walked around the counter "Can you talk?" Taylor said in a low voice. "Yes, give me a minute," Zoe answered.

She took Mr. Jackson's order from the window and walked over to get the coffee pot. She poured Mr. Jackson coffee and then walked back over to Taylor. "What's up?"

"My father's going crazy."

"I told you he wasn't going to like the idea of you and Anton. I told you from the beginning. And it's all over town too. You know Linda was at Leo's last night, and she can't keep anything to herself."

"What's so wrong with Anton?" Taylor asked defensively. "Nothing if you want a thug and a wannabe gangster." "He's not that bad," Taylor said sadly.

"Taylor! He beats his women. That's his and Mike's MO." "I don't think Anton will ever hit me," Taylor said.

Just then, Anton, Mike, and Frank walked through the door. Mike and Frank took a seat at the booth by the door, and Anton walked over to Taylor. Zoe look at Anton and then Taylor.

"Speaking of the devil," Zoe said.

Anton frowned at her and turned his attention to Taylor.

"Hi, baby," he said as he leaned over and kissed her on the cheek.

"Hi, Anton," Taylor said with a smile.

"Did you eat?" Anton asked. "No," Taylor said.

"Well do you want to eat with us?" Anton asked, pointing at the booth where Mike and Frank were.

"Sure," Taylor said as she stood up.

They then walked over to the booth together. Frank got up, walked to the other side, and sat down by Mike. Anton motioned for Taylor to sit down, and then he sat beside her.

"Hi, Taylor," Frank said as he looked down at his menu. "Hi, Frank. Hi, Mike," Taylor said.

"Whatever," Mike said, looking out the window.

Anton handed Taylor a menu. "Order whatever you'd like. It's on me." "Thank you," Taylor said, feeling special.

Zoe walked over. "Whenever you are ready, just call me. I'll take your order." Mike and Frank looked at each other. "We are ready," they said. "Could you give me second, guys?" Anton said, frustrated. "What would you like, Taylor?"

"I'll take a double cheeseburger and some fries," Taylor said. "Make that two," said Mike.

"Make it three," Frank said.

"I'll try the chicken Parmesan," said Anton. "That comes with a soup or salad," said Zoe. "What kind of soup do you have?" Anton asked. "Tomato."

"I'll take the salad."

"What kind of dressing would you like?" "Ranch."

"Anything to drink with that?" Zoe asked. "A Pepsi for me," Taylor said

"I'll take a Pepsi too," said Frank. "I'll take a coffee," Mike said.

"Just water for me, and can I have lemon slices for my water and a straw?" Anton asked.

"Coming up."

Anton put his arm around Taylor and pulled her close to him.

"So how was your day?" he asked, looking into her eyes.

"It started out great," Taylor said. "I went to class and then to work. But then ..." She stopped and looked out the window.

Anton looked at Taylor. "Then what?" he asked, concerned. "It's nothing. Don't worry about it," Taylor said.

"Tell me," Anton pleaded.

"It's my father. He's not too happy about this." "About what?" Anton asked.

"About us."

"Well it's not like we are breaking any laws," Anton said angrily. "You are an adult. You make your own decisions." He looked at Taylor, pleased with himself that he was getting under the sheriff's skin. Things were going just like he wanted them to.

"I wish it was that simple," Taylor said sadly.

"Let me ask you a question," Anton said seriously. "Look at me so I can see your pretty little eyes." Taylor looked at Anton.

"Do you want to be with me?" he asked her.

"Oh, brother," Mike said as he rolled his eyes and looked out the window. "What do you mean by that?" Taylor asked.

"You know what I mean. Do you want to be my girl?"

Taylor blushed, and her face turned red. "Yes," she said in a low voice. Anton's eyes sparkled as he smiled. "Then we won't let anything get in our way. The hell with your father, and the hell with the whole San Juan County Sheriff's Department."

"You're starting something, Anton," Mike said. "We don't need this shit right now ... not right now."

"This is my business," Anton said.

"How is this your business when you are involving us?" Mike said. "How am I involving you?" Anton yelled loudly.

"Come on, you guys. Calm down. Mike's right, Anton," Frank said. "Shut up, Frank," Anton said.

"I'm just letting you know," Frank said, backing down.

"I don't want to drive a wedge between you and your buddies," Taylor said, concerned.

"Don't worry about it. They'll be okay," Anton said.

Zoe walked over with their order. "A double cheeseburger for you, Taylor, and you, Mike. And a double cheeseburger for you Frank, and a salad and a chicken Parmesan for you, Anton. Two Pepsis, a coffee, and water."

"Are there refills on the Pepsi?" Frank asked. "Yes," Zoe answered. "Would that be all?"

Just then, Jonathan and Alex walked into the diner. They stood and waited for Zoe to seat them. Jonathan looked around the diner and saw Taylor sitting with Anton. His heart dropped, and a lump grew in his throat. He tapped Alex on the shoulder and pointed to Taylor and Anton.

Alex's eyes widened. "That bitch," he said. Zoe walked over to Jonathan and Alex. "Are you ready to be seated?" "Yes," said Jonathan.

She led them to a booth across from Taylor's. They walked past Taylor and Anton. Taylor looked up and saw Jonathan, and then she began to feel bad. Jonathan looked as Anton put his arm around Taylor.

He wanted to jump up and say something, but he just sat there.

"I can't believe this," Alex said. "That tramp."

"Don't talk about her like that," Jonathan said angrily.

"But she's with that no-good, son of a bitch Anton. That tramp." "Don't say that," Jonathan said again. "She's still my friend."

Jonathan and Alex looked at Anton and Mike as they yelled out loud. "Man, she wants to be with them characters? If I were you, I'd forget about her. She's a scumbag," Alex said.

"Don't talk about her like that. You've known her practically all your life. I just have to talk to her. That's all." Zoe walked over to Jonathan and Alex.

"I'll have a double cheeseburger and a chocolate shake," Jonathan said. "Make that two," Alex said.

Taylor then looked at Jonathan. Jonathan looked at Taylor, and their eyes met. Anton looked over at Jonathan, put his arm around Taylor, and pulled her close. Jonathan became angry, dropped his head, and began playing with his phone.

"Do you want to go to the movies, Taylor?" Anton asked.

"It's getting late. What do you want to see?" "There's a new Batman movie out."

"Okay."

"Do you want to go, Frank?" Anton asked. "No. I better get home," Frank said.

"Me too," said Mike.

Anton walked over to the register and paid the check. Taylor dropped her head to avoid looking at Jonathan as she walked over to Anton. They walked out of the door. Jonathan watch them get into Anton's car, and his heart melted. Alex just shook his head and continued eating.

Chapter 9

SHERIFF MURPHY WAS in his room lying across the bed in his T-shirt and jeans. The house was dark and quiet, and he could hear every sound the house made. He could hear the floor cracking and the soft rumble of the air conditioner. He was too angry to sleep. He just lay there and closed his eyes.

He looked at the clock and saw it was 12:59 a.m., and a rage rose inside of him. Taylor hadn't made it home yet, and she was out with that no-good Anton, doing who knows what. He wanted to put the chain on the door but said to himself he was going to let her in.

He thought about the time he arrested Anton for robbing the liquor store. He still had the gun on him that he'd hit the clerk on the head with. The clerk needed fifteen stitches as a result. Anton didn't try to hide. He just drove around town with the evidence in his car.

How stupid could you be? Murphy thought. *Anton is no good, and he will always be no good.*

Suddenly, his heart dropped. *What if she gets pregnant? What am I going to do if Taylor has a baby out of wedlock? What would my friends say? We've always had a good reputation in this town, and now she's going to ruin all of that. How could she do this to me?*

Sheriff Murphy heard the front door open and then shut. He could hear Taylor tiptoeing across the living room floor. He was outraged as he looked at the clock as saw it was two o'clock in the morning. Taylor had to get up in the morning and go to school, which he paid for. He jumped up, stormed into the living room, and turned on the light.

Taylor was stunned and frightened as she watched her father march into the room.

"Where in the hell have you been all night, Taylor Murphy?" "Anton and I went to a movie," she explained.

"That theater closed at midnight!"

"Then we just drove around and talked, Daddy."

"Don't lie to me!" the sheriff yelled as his face began to turn red. "You out there tramping around with that no-good son of a bitch Anton."

"We didn't do anything, Daddy. We just talked." "What are people going to say?"

"I don't care what people say."

"That's your problem, Taylor," he snapped. "You don't know how it feels to be talked about by the whole town you're living in. Just wait, and you'll see how people can be. You're going to have to move. Are you going to school today?"

"Yes."

"It's already two o'clock," the sheriff pointed out. "I'll get up," Taylor said, trying to reassure him. "Why can't you see Anton for what he is?!" he yelled "Anton is a good person, Daddy."

"Anton is scum ... a criminal. You are a pretty girl. You can have any boy in this town. What about Jonathan?"

"I don't want any boy, Daddy. Jonathan is nice, but I don't like him like that."

"How can I make you see that Anton is making a fool out of you?!" Sheriff Murphy yelled.

Taylor backed up, and tears formed in her eyes.

"And when he gets through using you, he is going to drop you like a hot potato!" he continued. "What are you going to do then? No one will want you then! Jonathan won't be interested in you anymore! What are you going to do? Tell me!"

Taylor shook her head. "It won't be like that, Daddy," she cried out.

"If you continue to see that boy, you're going to have to leave here, because I'm not going to watch you throw your life away over some scum like Anton! And I'm through paying your tuition too! I paid this semester! You figure out how you are going to pay for next semester!" he yelled.

"But I only have one more semester to go," she cried.

"Figure it out, Taylor." Sheriff Murphy then turned away, walked to his room, and slammed the door.

"Daddy!" Taylor cried out as she sat on the couch with her head in her hands. She wanted to go to her room, but she was scared to lie down. She had never seen her father act like that before, and the things he said were unbelievable. She sat on the couch until it was almost time for her dad to go to work and then tiptoed to her room and closed the door. She could hear her father moving around getting ready for work. She heard him stop by her door several times as he moved along the hall. He finally opened the front door and slammed it shut.

Taylor looked at her clock. It was six thirty. She jumped up, ran into the bathroom, and turned on the shower. She could still hear her father yelling. "Anton is making a fool out of you." His words lingered in her head all day.

Chapter 10

JONATHAN AND ALEX walked into Roscoe's, a bar in downtown Austin. Jonathan eyes sparkled and gleamed, and his pulse pounded when he saw the number of arcade games in the room. There were pool tables, arcade games, pinball machines … they had everything he could dream of, including a dance floor. Jonathan grinned and hooted when he saw the DJ and the number of pretty girls walking around the place.

The friends found a table in the back and motioned for the waiter. Jonathan sat back in his chair so he could take in the sites of this enormous place. He looked past the bar at the row of arcade games, and to his amazement, he spotted his favorite game: Daytona USA. He loved racing games and owned every racing game he could find, including Need for Speed, Race Driver Grid, and SSX Tricky, just to name a few. Jonathan tapped Alex on the shoulder and pointed to the game.

"All right," Alex said. Alex shared his friend's love for arcade games. Just then, the waitress walked over to them. "I will be your waitress," she said. "Here are two menus."

"Can you give us a second?" Jonathan asked.

The waitress walked away, and Jonathan watched her as she walked toward a row of tables nearby. Suddenly, his eyes glared, his teeth clenched, and his fist tightened until his knuckles turned white.

"That bastard," he said.

"What's going on?" Alex asked.

Jonathan pointed to a table two rows in front of them.

"That sly dog. Well, you know Anton gets all the girls," Alex said with a chuckle.

"That's not funny, Alex," Jonathan said. "He's supposed to be with Taylor." "Well, you know what he's going to say—what guys like him always say.

He's not married to her."

Jonathan shook his head in horror as he watched Anton smooch all over a redheaded girl.

"She's not even all that cute," Jonathan said. "She's fat and has freckles. Taylor would run circles around her." "Anton is the ultimate player," Alex said.

"No, he's making a fool out of my friend." Jonathan picked up his phone and snapped Anton's picture.

"Wait a minute ... What are you going to do with that?" Alex asked.

"I'm going to show Taylor. A photo is worth a thousand words."

The waitress came back. "Are you ready to order?" she asked.

"Yes, I'm starving. I'll have a nacho supreme and a Sprite," Alex said.

"I'll have a double cheeseburger and a Coke," said Jonathan.

"Coming up."

The waitress walked away, and Jonathan looked at the redheaded fat girl squealing out a laugh.

"If I'm going to be a player, I'm going to play with pretty girls," Jonathan said. "Big girls need love too," laughed Alex.

The DJ put on a dance beat, and Anton and the fat girl stood up to dance. She squealed out another laugh, and Anton held her in his arms.

"Oh my God ... Did you feel the floor move?" Jonathan said. "Come on. She's not that big," Alex said.

"Yes, she is she's enormous. No wonder he's here in Austin, because he didn't want his pals to see her in San Juan. I should take a video and post it on the internet."

"You wouldn't," Alex said with a gasp.

"I will. Let him fuck with me," Jonathan said as he recorded the pair dancing. "The guys are going to get a kick out of this."

"You are sick, Jonathan."

"No. He's messing around on Taylor."

Soon, the waitress came back with their food. "Will that be all?" she said.

"Yes," Alex said as he began to attack his nachos.

Jonathan watched as Anton kissed the fat redheaded girl on the mouth. "How could he? Who is she? I've never seen her around here."

"Maybe she lives here in Austin," Alex said Anton and the redheaded girl sat down.

"Good. The mini quake is over," Jonathan said. "You have a problem," Alex said.

Jonathan watched in amazement as the redheaded girl fed Anton his fries and wiped his mouth.

"They act like they have been together for years," Jonathan said. "Wouldn't it be funny if that were his wife?" Alex said, laughing.

"No, that's just some poor slob Anton is using like he uses all the girls back home."

"I wonder what she has that he wants," Alex said.

"Money. You know what guys like Anton want. This whole night is on her. Anton, the male escort, the male gigolo," Jonathan said

"She's paying a high price to be with Anton tonight," Alex said.

Jonathan and Alex finished their food and made their way to the Daytona USA arcade game. Jonathan watched as Anton and the redheaded girl played pool. Anton leaned over her to show her how to hold the pool cue. She hit the cue ball, missed her shot, and let out a squeal.

Alex went first on the game. He played with such precision and form that his car came in second at the finish line. When it was Jonathan's turn, his heart raced, and his knees became week. He imagined he was in a real car on the race track—no one but him and the drive. He could lose himself in the game. There was no one to bother him—no schoolwork, no parents, no Anton, no Taylor, just him and his car. This was the one thing he could do well, and he enjoyed every moment he got to play.

His car finished first, and he advanced to the next level with a harder track, but it didn't matter. There wasn't a track too difficult for him to race on. He imagined that he was in the real Daytona 500, driving against some of the best drivers in the world. What if he could win the Daytona 500? Taylor would like him then, and they'd get married—race driver Jonathan and his amazing wife, Taylor. But now the girl of his dreams wanted to be with that idiot Anton.

Soon it was Alex's turn. Jonathan got up and looked over at Anton who was playing Ms. Pac-Man. He was showing off for his lady friend. She hugged him around the waist as he played. Jonathan realized that after all this time, Anton hadn't noticed them. *I wonder what he would do if he knew we saw him here*, Jonathan thought. *If I tell Taylor, what would he say?*

The redhead let out another squeal as Anton whispered in her ear. Jonathan looked in disgust and then in amazement it was the redheaded girl's turn to play. She moved Ms. Pac-Man through the maze, squealing as she went along, and to Jonathan's amazement, she made it to the second level. Anton clapped, and she squealed.

Alex had also made it to the next level. His score was almost as high as Jonathan's. Jonathan knew he had to pay attention, or Alex would beat him, and he couldn't let that happen. He was the race car driver. Jonathan looked at the time. It was twelve thirty. They had to drive home—his mother would be worried, as she knew he was in Austin.

"Let's play one more game before we have to go," he told Alex.

The two friends looked over at Anton who was playing Super Mario Bros. The redheaded girl looked worn out, and her squealing had stopped. Jonathan and Alex played Asteroids. Jonathan was good at that game too, but he did not care for it like he did Daytona 500. They played a couple levels and then got ready to go. Jonathan looked over at Anton who was getting ready to go as well.

"Let's let Anton know we were here," Jonathan said as they walked toward him.

"No. Let's just go," Alex said. "You have your video. He can't deny that. Let him have his fun."

As they walked to the door, Jonathan looked around for the last time. Just before he walked out, he looked back at Anton who was getting ready to go and then looked at the redheaded girl.

"Nope. There is no denying this," he said as he walked out of the door.

He headed for the car, thinking about how he was going to tell Taylor.

Chapter 11

TAYLOR FINISHED TAKING Mr. Sanchez's blood pressure and temperature. "You can go back to the waiting area and wait for the doctor to call you," she said as he rolled down his sleeve and stepped out the door. Taylor entered the information in the computer and sipped on a cup of coffee. She looked at the time and saw it was three o'clock. Taylor had thirty minutes left. She couldn't wait to go home and get out of her work clothes.

She was meeting Anton later that night, and they were going to a horror film festival. Taylor loved horror movies. She loved snuggling up on the couch at night with all the lights out to watch the movies on television. Her father loved movies as well, and every year they would go to the Pontiac Theater to watch the film festival. But this year Anton asked her to go with him. It was just as well, because her father wasn't speaking to her much these days.

He would come home, eat his dinner, and then head to the living room to watch the baseball playoffs until he fell asleep. He went to bed early and woke up and left early. Taylor didn't try to have a conversation with him. She just spent all her time trying to stay out of his way.

Taylor had asked Zoe if she wanted to go to the festival, but Zoe had to work a double at the diner. So, it was just going to be Taylor and Anton. She liked Anton and enjoyed every moment they spent together, which wasn't a lot since she had to work full time now and go to school. She had to pay her own tuition next semester, so she had to save up as much money as she could. *A small price to pay to be with the man of my dreams*, she thought.

"You have one more patient," Miss Martinez said as she stuck her head through the door.

"I'll be there in a second," Taylor said as she closed out Mr. Sanchez's file. Taylor went out into the waiting area and called Mrs. Hudson, an older African American woman who suffered from diabetes and high blood pressure Mrs. Hudson got up and slowly walked to the back.

"Have you been cutting back on all the salt, Mrs. Hudson?" Taylor asked

"I've tried, but it's hard. Food tastes so bland without it."

"You will get used to it." Taylor wrapped the blood pressure cuff around Mrs. Hudson's arm and stuck the electric thermometer in her mouth. The blood pressure machine registered 120/70.

"Good. Your blood pressure is normal, and your temperature is good too. You can go take a seat in the waiting area and wait for the doctor to call you," Taylor said.

"Thank you," Mrs. Hudson said as she slowly walked out the door. Taylor finished up and turned off the computer. She drank the last of her coffee before grabbing her purse and heading for the entrance.

"Got a hot date tonight?" Miss Martinez asked as Taylor passed her.

"Yes. I'll tell you all about it Tuesday." Taylor said.

*****

The line outside the Pontiac Theater was filled with inpatient, hungry young adults who were eager to watch the five greatest horror movies of all time. Anton hugged Taylor around the waist as they eagerly stood in line.

"How was your week?" he asked as he looked down into her eyes.

"It was okay. I had to work a double last Friday. That's why I couldn't go with you to Austin."

"That's okay," Anton said nervously. "I had to finish up at the garage anyway."

"Maybe we could go some other time?" Taylor asked

"Look ... They are showing *The Exorcist*," he said, trying to change the subject.

"Yeah, that's one of my favorite movies."

"Mine too."

Just then, Mike and Frank walked up. "Hey, Taylor," they both said. Then Tammy and Ashley ran over.

Anton quickly pulled Mike to the side. "You brought Tammy and Ashley? You know they can't keep anything to themselves."

"Relax," Mike told him. "They are not going to blow your cover." Tammy and Ashley stood by Taylor in line.

"That's a nice blouse," said Ashley. "Thank you," Taylor said.

Anton hurried up and stood by Taylor.

"Have you ever been to Roscoe's, Taylor?" Ashley asked. Tammy laughed. Anton gave Ashley a mean look.

"Taylor, they are showing *The Exorcism of Emily Rose* as well," he quickly said, trying to change the subject.

"That's a really scary one. I don't think I'll be able to sleep." "I'll protect you."

The doors opened, and the usher began to take their tickets. Anton and Taylor went into the theater. It was a historic building with gold and maroon walls, large gold columns, a grand staircase leading to the balcony, a large chandelier hanging from the ceiling, and maroon carpet covering the floor.

"Want some popcorn?" Anton asked as he grabbed Taylor by the hand, trying to separate from Frank and Mike.

"Sure," Taylor said.

"Good," Anton told her. "We'll get a big bucket with lots of butter." They walked up to the concession stand where Taylor spotted Jonathan buying some nachos. "Hi, Jonathan," she said.

Jonathan turned around and looked surprised to see Anton standing next to Taylor. Anton's heart dropped when he saw the look on Jonathan's face. He had seen Jonathan and Alex at Roscoe's last Friday night but had pretended that he didn't. He began to worry that Jonathan was going to tell Taylor about his redheaded companion.

"Hi, Taylor," Jonathan said.

"I didn't know that you liked to go see horror movies," Taylor said.

"I wouldn't miss it for the world," Jonathan said with a smile.

Anton grabbed Taylor and hurried up to the counter so they could order their popcorn. Jonathan walked over to Alex who was waiting at the entrance of the auditorium.

"That scum," Jonathan said. "He saw us at Roscoe's." "How do you know?" Alex asked.

"Because I could read it all over his face."

Jonathan and Alex watched as Anton bought Taylor some popcorn and a Coke. Anton looked over at Jonathan and tried to lose himself in the crowd. Everyone went into the auditorium and took their seats.

Alex and Jonathan sat down behind Anton and Taylor. Anton looked back at Jonathan and pulled Taylor closer. Jonathan clenched his teeth and rolled his eyes, trying to focus on the big screen in front of him.

Anton thought of the redheaded girl who he'd taken out last Friday. She was just a girl he'd met a couple of months earlier. He was just her friend. It didn't mean anything, and he'd just asked her out because Taylor declined and had to work. She was just a friend, and he figured he'd tell Taylor if Jonathan said anything. He began to fidget in his seat. *Why do I feel this way if I don't really care for Taylor?* he thought.

The movie started, and the audience cheered as the lights dimmed. Taylor grabbed on to Anton and held him tight. Anton's heart fluttered, and a tingling feeling went through him. He grinned from ear to ear.

Jonathan rolled his eyes and clenched his teeth as he watched Taylor hold on to Anton. *That bastard. He doesn't deserve her*, Jonathan thought as Anton grabbed on to Taylor. During every suspenseful part of the movie, Taylor would jump and grab Anton. Jonathan began to feel sick as he realized that Taylor was happy with Anton, and Anton wasn't going to go away. It would probably take a lot to get Taylor away from Anton, but he was going to try. He looked at the screen and realized he had missed the entire movie.

Anton held on tightly to Taylor. *She is pretty. Any man would be glad to have her*, he thought. He then remembered Jonathan was sitting behind them. *Jonathan may be interested, but she's with me.*

Taylor looked at Anton and snuggled up against him as he watched the movie. She thought about how great things were going. If only her father could see how Anton treated her, then he wouldn't be so angry. She thought about Jonathan and felt bad that there weren't two of her. But she had to make a choice, and she had chosen Anton. Anton was handsomer, but then again, Jonathan was handsome too. They both were—in their own ways. But Jonathan was too nice, too safe. Anton had some mystery about him.

The last movie was almost over.

"You want some chocolate?" Anton said. "I'm going to get us some candy bars and another Coke. I have to stretch my legs." He got up and walked up the aisle to the exit.

Jonathan watched as Anton left the auditorium and then leaned over. "Are you enjoying yourself?" he asked Taylor.

"Yes, thank you," Taylor said.

"Shh," a woman from the back said.

"They showed some pretty good movies this year." "They did," Taylor said.

"Shut up!" the women yelled from back.

Jonathan sat back and began watching the movie again.

Anton came back with a couple of giant Hershey bars and a large Coke with two straws. At the end of the last movie, the lights came up, and everyone began to clap.

Anton stood up and stretched. "Did you enjoy yourself?" he asked Taylor. "Yes, I did," she told him.

"Are you hungry? We can go to the diner and grab an early breakfast." "Okay."

Taylor stood up, and they began to move toward the exit. Jonathan and Alex were in front as the crowd spilled out onto the sidewalk. Anton grabbed Taylor by the hand, and they began walking toward the diner. Taylor looked at the time on the bank building's clock and saw it was 3:20 a.m. and sixty-seven degrees. A cool breeze was in the air, and Anton put his jacket around her shoulders as they walked down the street. The crowd followed them. It seemed everybody had the same idea to get a bite to eat, and the diner was the only place open this early Taylor and Anton stood in line outside the diner waiting for a table. Taylor could see the waiter running around trying to wait on everyone.

"For Halloween, do you want to go to Blanco?" Anton asked. "They have this awesome haunted house. They say it's so scary no one has ever made it through."

"Sure," Taylor said. "I'd love to go." She looked ahead and saw Jonathan and Alex were also waiting to get inside. Taylor couldn't wait to be seated.

She wanted a big stack of blueberry pancakes and a tall glass of orange juice.

Chapter 12

THE BOWLING ALLEY was crowded for a Friday evening, and every lane was taken. Jonathan and Alex had gotten there just in time to get one. They paid for ten frames. Alex went first, while Jonathan took score. He picked up the ball and rolled it down the lane. All the pins fell, and he jumped and yelled, "Strike."

Jonathan just shook his head, because he knew it was going to be one of those days. Alex was a good bowler. In fact, he was great at all sports.

"Top that," Alex said as he returned to his seat.

Jonathan grabbed his ball, took a deep breath, moved toward the lane, and rolled it. Every pin but two fell. He jumped as though he was going to make the other pins fall, but they didn't. He grabbed his ball again, took a deep breath, and rolled his ball. It missed the other pins and went into the back of the lane.

"You'll get them next time, buddy," Alex said as he wrote down the score. "Hey, Jonathan. Check that out."

Jonathan looked over toward the entrance and saw Anton, Frank, and Mike, along with Tammy and Ashley. They had walked up to the counter and were paying for a lane, while the girls picked out shoes. Anton had his own bowling ball.

"Don't mind them," Jonathan said as he sat down to take score. "Where is Taylor?" asked Alex, noticing that Taylor wasn't with them. Jonathan didn't look up. He didn't want them to notice he was watching them. They had been assigned to the lane next to theirs, and Mike sat down and began to take score. Anton went first. He positioned himself like a professional, rolled his ball down the lane, and scored a strike. The girls cheered as he sat down between them. Frank stood up to take his turn next.

Alex got up and grabbed his ball. "Let me show them how it's done," he mumbled.

Jonathan positioned himself, took a deep breath, and rolled his ball. He also scored a strike.

Jonathan and Alex could hear everything Mike, Frank, and Anton were talking about. At first, they were talking about a football game between the Cowboys and the Bears. Then Frank asked Anton why he hadn't brought Taylor bowling with him.

"I'm not going to take that bitch everywhere with me," Anton answered. Jonathan looked over at him.

"I'm only going to tap that a couple of times, and then I'm going to dump that bitch."

Alex looked at Jonathan, who became angry as he watched Anton high-five Mike.

"I don't see why you are talking to her anyway. She thinks she's too good for us," Tammy said.

"Yeah, all of them whores on the east end do," Ashley said Frank pointed to Jonathan and Alex. "The whole east end," she continued.

Jonathan grabbed his ball and motioned before rolling his ball down the lane. He bowled another strike. He wanted to leave, find Taylor, and shake her until she came to her senses, but he thought if he told her what Anton was saying, she wouldn't believe him. Anton and Mike made cracks about the sheriff and Taylor all night. Jonathan listened and watched how obscene they were acting—like they didn't care about anything.

Alex shook his head. "I should tell the sheriff what they were saying," he said.

"They are out to hurt Taylor. We have to talk to her, Alex," Jonathan said "Do you have her number?"

"Yes. Let's go to the concession stand and give her a call," Jonathan said. The pair headed to the concession area and found a table. A group of kids were celebrating a birthday at the table next to theirs, and the whole place was noisy. The children were running around, crying, and blowing party horns.

"Let's step outside," Jonathan said. "I can't hear through the noise." They walked to the exit and stepped outside. The night air was warm on Jonathan's arms as he looked for Taylor's number in his phone. The area was quiet compared to the bowling alley. All he could hear were cars passing by on the street outside the bowling alley.

He found Taylor's number and dialed it. "Hello?" Taylor answered in a low, sweet voice. "Taylor, this is Jonathan."

Taylor was quiet for a second and then said, "Oh. Hi, Jonathan." "Where are you? We have to talk," Jonathan said.

"Oh, I'm at work. I had to take an extra shift this week. I might be working full time from now on."

"When would be a good time to talk to you?"

"I don't know. I have to work," Taylor told him. "Maybe Tuesday after class?"

"It's urgent, Taylor."

"I'll be busy till then Tuesday after class."

Jonathan became upset but just said, "Okay. I'll see you then." "Okay. I have to go," she said as she hung up the phone.

"What did she say?" Alex asked as he noticed the frustration on Jonathan's face.

"She had to work an extra shift at the hospital and can't talk till Tuesday."

"She can't, or she won't?" Alex said angrily. "What are you going to do now?"

"I don't know, but I will think of something. I swear on my grandmother's grave: if Anton does anything to hurt, Taylor I'll kill him. I don't care how crazy he's supposed to be."

Chapter 13

THE SUNLIGHT SHONE through the smudged windows of the diner, filling the room and taking over the dim light that glowed from the light fixtures on the ceiling. The empty booths that nestled against the windows had once been filled with hungry and impatient customers. The long counter was still cluttered with dirty white dishes, and the stools along the counter were now deserted.

Zoe hurried and cleaned the counter. She wiped tirelessly at the coffee stains with a soapy, dingy dish towel. She placed napkins in the empty napkin holders and filled the salt and paper shakers. She walked around the diner and collected all the laminated menus that offered dinner foods, as well as pancakes, burgers, and meatloaf.

She placed ketchup and mustard on each table and placed two lemon meringue pies under glass dome displays. Zoe's shoulder dropped, and her chest caved in as she brought a shaky hand to her forehead. "I have to take a breather," she said to herself.

Zoe walked over to the jukebox and played one of her favorite Katy Perry songs. She collapsed in a booth near the jukebox in the back of the diner. Her feet pulsated, and her body began to unravel from the tenseness of the afternoon. As Zoe listened to Katy Perry's voice, her pulse slowed, her body became calm, her breathing grew shallow, her eyes began to close, and her nerves settled. And she welcomed the new feeling that she now had, because she had been tense all day.

The song played, and Zoe floated with the music and imagined she was a million miles away. She began to think of the relaxation exercises her mother used to practice when she was a little girl. She and her mother would lie on the floor and listen to a cassette tape of a well-known psychiatrist who would explain the relaxation techniques.

"Lie on the floor," the cassette would say. "Feel your body sinking like you are on a beach lying in the sand. Feel your feet sinking in the sand. Now your legs ... now your body." Zoe imagined that she was sinking in the sand on a secluded beach in Hawaii. She began to relax. If only the diner could stay empty for the rest of her shift.

She felt the music calming her, and her feet no longer tingled. She began to fall into a very light sleep. Zoe imagined the hot sun shining on her face as she lay effortlessly on the beach ... Suddenly, the songs stopped, and the bell on the door rang.

More hungry customers, she thought as she got up to work through her tiresome shift. Zoe looked over at the door. It was Mr. Jackson. He'd been a regular at the diner since his wife had become sick. They had lived in San Juan for more than thirty years. He and his wife were inseparable, and people felt they were the perfect couple. He always had a kind word to say about his wife. And then a year ago she had been diagnosed with dementia. She deteriorated fast, and he was forced to put her in a home. After that, he began frequenting the diner, as there were no more home-cooked meals.

"Hi, Mr. Jackson," Zoe said as she motioned for him to take a seat. "I'll sit at the counter if you don't mind," he said, smiling.

"No, I don't mind at all." Zoe gave him a menu.

"What will it be today, sir?" she asked as she forced a smile.

"I think I'll try the meatloaf," he said, handing her back the menu. "What would you like to drink?"

"Coffee, black—you know how I like it," he said.

"I just made a new pot," Zoe said. "Coming right up."

She took the order and put it in the window, so Max could prepare the meatloaf. She then poured a steaming cup of fresh coffee.

"How was school today?" Mr. Jackson asked.

"It was fine. I have one more semester. My clinicals are going well too." "That's good ... Going to be a nurse, are you?"

"Sure am. In a few short months, I will be an RN."

"That's excellent. Are you going to stay here in town?" Mr. Jackson questioned.

"No. I want to be an army nurse," Zoe explained. "I've been talking to a recruiter, but I haven't really made up my mind. If not, I'm thinking about moving to Dallas."

"Really? You should go for it. Be an army nurse ... See the world."

"Yeah," Zoe said.

"You know, I was in the army. Did one of my first tours in 1967 in Vietnam. I saw a lot of combat. Went there three times in 1967, '69, and '70. I was one of the lucky ones. A lot of my friends didn't make it back. But you will be great. This is a great time for women to be in the military. You'll get a lot of opportunities. You can go far."

"I know," Zoe said. "It's just my mother ... She worries about me."

"Well you can't live under your mother forever."

Zoe got Mr. Jackson's food, poured him another cup of coffee, and went back to the jukebox.

"Do you still have 'California Girls' by the Beach Boys in there, Zoe?" Mr. Jackson asked.

"I think so."

"Could you play it? It was one of my wife's favorite songs. We used to play it a lot when I got home from the war."

"I sure will," Zoe said. She found the song and played it. She sat down and tried to lose herself in the music just as the door opened once again. It was Mrs. Armstrong. Mrs. Armstrong was new in town. She and her husband had six kids, and one of her daughters was just old enough to work at the diner. Mrs. Armstrong has inquired to Jack about a week earlier about a position, but he was too busy to get back to her.

"Is Jack in?" Mrs. Armstrong asked Zoe as she walked up to the counter. "No, I'm sorry. He stepped out. He won't be back for another hour." "Do you know if he filled the opening yet?" she asked nervously.

"No, not yet. The job is still open."

"Good. My girl needs that job. She has to help out since Fred got laid off and all. Things are getting a little tight."

"I see," Zoe said. "Do you want anything?"

"I'll have a piece of pie and a cup of coffee while I wait. Do you mind if I sit over there?" she asked, pointing to the back near the window.

"No, I don't mind."

Mrs. Armstrong went over to the booth and sat down. Zoe brought her a cup of coffee and a big piece of lemon meringue pie. The Beach Boy's song had finished playing, and Zoe started another Katy Perry song before sitting back down. She looked at the clock—two hours to go, and her feet were beginning to go numb.

Jonathan and Alex tapped on the window to get Zoe's attention. She looked up at the window, Jonathan motioned for her to come outside. She stood up, walked to the door, and stepped out onto the sidewalk. The air was warm on her face as the sun began to set behind the hills. She walked up to Jonathan, who was clenching his jaw. He began speaking through his teeth with forced restraint while talking with his hands.

"Where is Taylor?" he asked.

"I don't know," Zoe told him. "I think she's at work."

"Do you know if she's serious about Anton—that bastard?" "I told you at school that she's serious about that jerk."

"I have to tell you about some of the things he has been saying—"

"And doing," Alex said, interrupting.

"She's your girl. Maybe if you tell her about what I'm going to tell you, she'll listen," Jonathan said.

"I try not to pry in Taylor's affairs. She doesn't want to hear my opinion; besides, everybody knows how Anton is," Zoe said.

"Except Taylor," Alex pointed out.

"You've got to do something. You can't stand around and let your girl go down like that," Jonathan said.

"What exactly did Anton do that made you so upset?" Zoe asked. Jonathan began to tell Zoe how he saw Anton in Austin with another girl. Then they were at the bowling alley, and Anton said he was going to use Taylor and then dump her. Zoe asked Jonathan and Alex to come in and have a seat in the diner. Jonathan showed Zoe the video and told her all the things Anton had said about Sheriff Murphy. Zoe listened with horror as Jonathan told her all about the night before. She couldn't believe what she was hearing. She knew Anton was a wannabe player, but she didn't know he was a scumbag.

"If I tell Taylor that, she won't believe me. She'll just think I am another person dumping on Anton," Zoe said. "I love Taylor like she's like my sister. I don't want to hurt her or lose her friendship."

"But you won't be a friend if you sit around and let Anton hurt her," Alex said. "What you say might hurt her, but she will come around and will love you even more after she sees the truth."

"Tell her I have something she need to see," Jonathan said. "I will show her the video."

"What I should do is tell Sheriff Murphy. He'll know what to do," Zoe said. "This makes me angry. Taylor needs a good shaking. We should just shake her until she gets her senses back."

"We'll talk to her first before you say anything to the sheriff. If you tell her father, you will push her further away," Alex said.

"I know … I have to think about what I'm going to say and how I'm going to say it," Zoe said.

Chapter 14

ANTON LOWERED THE hood on Mr. Johnson's 2016 Toyota Camry. He had just finished up the oil change. He looked up at the sky and saw the sun was shining brightly. He had decided to go to Blanco State Park that day. He loved going to Blanco State Park. It was the closest thing to Yellowstone or the Grand Canyon he was going to get to. He always wanted to go to those places but never got the chance.

He thought about Taylor and how lucky she was that her aunt had taken her to Europe. He might not ever get to go to some of the places Taylor been. He couldn't stop thinking about Taylor. He felt bad about the things he had said about her last night; in fact, he felt lucky that Taylor liked him. And when they were together, he couldn't find it in his heart to hurt her.

But when he was around Mike and Frank, his mouth got in the way, and he had to keep his reputation. He was supposed to meet Taylor that night to take her to a state park, and he couldn't wait to take her. He couldn't think of anything else they could do. When you live in a small town, there isn't much to do. He couldn't wait to get off work and meet Taylor. He walked inside the garage, rolled down the garage door, and walked to the front of the store.

To his surprise, Deputy Jerry was waiting at the counter.

"I'm sorry, Deputy. I'm the only one here today. Steve called in sick. Have you been waiting long?" "No, I just walked in," Jerry said.

"How can I help you?"

"My tire is flat. I'm driving on my spare, and I want to look at your tires. I'm thinking about buying a new set."

"Sure. The tires we carry are on the wall over there. Let me look at your flat tire."

"Sure." The deputy rolled Anton the tire, and Anton took it in back. Jerry looked at the wall of tires and began reading the description on every one.

Anton walked out of the back and approached Jerry. "You see anything you like?"

"Yes. I think I'll go with Bridgestone."

"The Firestone are on sale," Anton said. "Buy two, get two free." "I think I better stick with Bridgestone." "You sure?" Anton questioned. "Yes."

"Okay, Bridgestone it is," Anton said.

"Do you have a minute?" Deputy Jerry asked. "I would like to talk to you." Anton looked at Jerry. He saw the look on Jerry's face and knew that whatever it was, it must be important.

"Give me a second to close up, and then we can go to the backroom." "Okay," Jerry said.

Anton closed up and then locked the front door and turn on the closed sign. Next, he walked to the back and locked the garage door. He went to the register, counted the money, and placed it in a safe in the back office. He came to the front and motioned for Jerry to come to the back.

Jerry walked to the back, and Anton led him to the break room. A small room with a table, a soda machine, and a vending machine, and a small refrigerator, and a microwave set on a counter and a flat-screen television hung on the wall. Anton took the remote and turned off the television.

"We can talk in here," Anton said, pointing to a chair at the table.

Jerry sat down and smiled at Anton.

Anton sat in the chair on the other side of the table.

"Anton, I don't want to take up much of your time, but I wanted to talk to you."

"Okay," Anton said.

"I see you and Taylor Murphy have been hanging out together. What's that all about?"

Anton's eyes widened, and then he got defensive. "What do you mean?" he asked. "What Taylor and I do is our business."

"I don't mean to upset you, Anton. I just want to know what your intentions are."

Anton looked at Jerry and thought about Sheriff Murphy. "Did the sheriff send you over here?"

"No," Jerry answered. "But Taylor is like a daughter to me, Anton, and I just want to know."

Anton let his guard down. "I asked Taylor to be my girl, and now we go together. I'm supposed to see her tonight."

"What are you going to do tonight?" Jerry asked.

"We are going to a state park. If we don't, I think we might just take in a movie."

"You want Taylor to be your girl, and you're serious about this? You're not just playing games?"

"No. I'm serious. I really like Taylor," Anton said. "Anything else?"

"Yes," Deputy Jerry said. "I haven't seen you in young adult service this year."

"I know. Those people don't want me there," Anton said. "No one in this town wants me anywhere around them. I see how those people in that church treat my mother."

"Treat your mother?" the deputy questioned. "Like she has leprosy … like she has a disease."

"Your mother is a very good person, and she's liked by everyone in the community."

Anton rolled his eyes. "That's not true."

"Anton, I know how these people feel about me, how the old ladies grab their purses when I walk past, and how people stop and stare when I come into the diner."

"Anton, you can't worry about what other people think. You have to go to church for yourself. If you act out because that's what people expect of you, then that's what people will always expect. But if you change and act differently, then that's what people will see and expect."

"It's not just the people in this town," Anton noted. "I don't think God wants me there. I've done too many bad things in my life."

"Anton, God knows you, and he knows your sins. He knew them before you were born. He knew your sins, my sins, the whole world's sins.

There's no sin too great that God can't forgive. Everyone in that church is a sinner. Read Romans 3:23 through 25 tonight when you get home."

Anton looked at Jerry and thought about his father's letter. *Maybe this is what my father was trying to say.*

Jerry looked at Anton. He saw that he was getting through to him. Anton made a mental note of what Jerry had told him to read: Romans 3:23–25.

"Okay, I'll read it, but I can't say for sure that I'll be at the young adult service on Sunday."

"Just read it, and if you have any questions, give me a call," Jerry said.

"I will," Anton assured him.

That didn't go so bad, Jerry thought as he got up and collected his things. "The tire will be ready for you tomorrow, Jerry," Anton said.

"Okay. I'll see you tomorrow."

Anton walked with him to the door. Jerry walked out, and Anton looked at his watch. *It's six o'clock*, he thought. *I have to go meet Taylor.*

Chapter 15

THE SKY WAS turning dark orange as the sun began to set behind the hills. There was a coolness in the air as the wind blew across Taylor's face, sending a chill through her body.

The air smelled of campfire and barbecue coals.

"We can sit here," Anton said, spreading out a blanket on the ground. "This is one of my favorite places to be."

"Mine too. My father used to bring me here to fish when I was a little girl," Taylor said.

"You know how to fish?" Anton asked, surprised.

"Yes. I used to fish a lot until I started college and work."

Anton looked at Taylor. His heart began to beat faster, and a good feeling came over him.

"I want to get my degree in nursing so my mother who is watching over me can be proud. She always wanted me to be a nurse. Then I think I'm going to move to Dallas."

"You're going to move to Dallas?" Anton asked.

"Yes," she said. "I hope so I want to get out of this town."

"I was thinking about moving to Dallas. I want to go back to school, but I don't know what I want to take up. Being a mechanic is pretty good, but I don't think I want to do that for the rest of my life," Anton said.

Taylor looked at Anton and noticed how gentle he was being—how he thought about his future like normal guys his age. She thought about her father and how wrong he was by saying that Anton had no ambition, that he was a thug and would always be a thug.

Anton noticed how Taylor was looking at him, and his heart skipped a beat. He was happy that Taylor was so infatuated with him. How could he do anything to hurt her? He felt shame for the things he was planning to do to her. He was a prick—but not a horrible prick.

He wanted Taylor to be his girl for as long as she would let him, no matter what people might say. It didn't matter. It was just between him and her. For as long as she was willing, he was willing. He wasn't going to let anyone stand in his way, and that included the sheriff.

The sun set completely, and the moon shone directly over the lake. The moonlight sparkled on the water, giving off a bright white glow. The crickets chirped, and Taylor could hear the sound of the leaves rustling in the trees from the wind.

"I love this place," Anton said. "Do you see how clear the sky is? You can see all the stars. I come here to stargaze and work out my problems. I love nature and animals. I have a chameleon at home. I used to have a snake, but it got to be a little too much for me ... That's what I think I want to do—go back to school and become a vet."

"You don't look like the type that would work with animals," Taylor said. "I'd rather work with animals than most people." Anton leaned over and kissed Taylor.

She wanted him to kiss her more, and she pulled him close as they kissed softly and passionately. Anton smelled good. His cologne mixed with the fragrance in the air made Taylor's head spin. She lost herself in the moment and never wanted to let him go.

Anton's heart jolted as he kissed her. It was the happiest he had been in a long time. *Why can't things be like this forever? Why can't the sheriff leave us alone?* he thought.

"You want to take a walk?" Taylor said, trying to break up the moment. She knew if she didn't stop, things would go too far.

Anton looked disappointed that Taylor had stopped, but he wanted to respect her and do things on her terms.

"Sure. I know a little spot you are going to love. I go there all the time. You've probably seen it. It's just over here—it's a great place to go fishing. We could do that one day. Maybe if your father comes around, he could come along."

"I hope so," Taylor said. "I'll pray that he does."

The couple stood up, and Anton folded the blanket.

"It's just over here," he said. Anton took her by the hand, and they walked slowly through the park along the lake until they reached a boat dock. Then they stepped up on the dock and walked to the end.

"That's my boat right there," Anton said, pointing to a beautiful white motorboat.

Taylor's eyes widened as she jumped up and down with excitement. "You have to take me on a ride!" she shouted.

"Okay. It's getting too late now, but I'll take you one day," Anton promised. "We'll make a day out of it. We better head back now. Do you want something to eat? Let's go to the diner."

Anton grabbed Taylor by the hand, and they walked slowly through the park back to the car. They drove to town listening to the radio. Anton thought about what Deputy Jerry said to him earlier, and he thought about his father.

Anton wanted to read the letter from his dad to make some sense out of it. *What does it all mean? Why should it matter to him? What does it have to do with this situation right now?* He wondered. But he couldn't tie the two together just yet.

Taylor sat quietly in the car listening to the radio. She had so much to tell Zoe. Maybe Zoe could go fishing with them one day too. *Her father would love to go*, she thought, *if Anton was Jonathan.* She just had to figure out how to get her father to come around—to see things the way she did. She knew that wasn't going to be easy.

They got out of the car and walked into the diner, which was so empty Zoe told them to take any seat. They sat in a booth next to the window, and Zoe brought them two menus.

"I'll just have a double cheeseburger and some fries and a vanilla shake," Taylor said.

"Me too," said Anton. "Coming up," Zoe said.

"What are you doing tomorrow?" Anton asked.

"I have to work tomorrow, but I get off at three o'clock."

"Do you want to take a drive to Austin? There's a club there called Club 57. It's usually crowded on weekends, but on Tuesdays, it's not so bad."

"I've never heard of that place," Taylor said.

"It's a nice place. They have a DJ and a dance floor, and we could have a couple of drinks."

"Okay," Taylor said. "I'd love to go. Are Frank and Mike going to be there?" "No, just us. I don't want those bums tagging along and ruining the fun." "Sure. It's a date then," Taylor said.

A minute later, Zoe brought them their food, and they ate.

Chapter 16

ANTON'S DAY WAS going great. He finally finished Mr. Holmes's car, and a steady flow of customers were coming into the shop. Mrs. Banks drove into the shop in her old 1978 Toyota Corolla.

"My car is making that noise again, Anton," she said. "Yes, Mrs. Banks. I'll look at it."

"Can you change my oil and give it a little wash too?" the woman asked. "Yes, ma'am," he said as she walked out of the garage.

Anton turned the ignition and listened. He looked and saw her check engine light was on. He popped the hood and examined a few things with the engine and immediately discovered the problem. He closed the hood, got back into the car, and drove it into the garage.

He went over to a black appointment book and scheduled Mrs. Banks's car to be the next on his list to work. He took out his phone and sent a text to Taylor: "How is it going?" "Really busy :(," she responded.

Anton laughed and then texted her back: "Poor baby." At the end of his text, he added a crying face emoji.

When he was done texting, Anton turned on the radio and began listening to Bruno Mars as he drank some water and ate an apple. He looked out of the door of the garage and noticed a black Lexus SUV pull up into the driveway. He looked inside and saw that it was Jonathan and his sidekick Alex. They got out of the SUV and walked into the garage.

Anton took a deep breath as he put down his apple.

He walked up to Jonathan. "May I help you?" he said, looking Jonathan straight in the eye and folding his arms across his chest.

Jonathan got angry and balled up his fist. "No, you can't help me, but you can help yourself!" Jonathan shouted. "First by leaving Taylor alone. I heard what you said at the bowling alley the other day! You don't mean Taylor any good. You're nothing but a rat!"

"Why are you so concerned? Why do you care what I say about Taylor?! What ... Do you like her? You want her to be your girl? Well she not; she's with me! What I say and do is none of your business!" Anton shouted back. "You don't want Taylor. You're just using her for your own little kicks," Jonathan shouted, becoming really angry. "That's what you do with all the girls—you use them—but Taylor won't be one of them."

"Why? Because you're going to save her? Taylor doesn't want to be with you! She's with the man she wants to be with. Get it through your yellow-haired head; besides, Taylor was with me last night—all night. We did things that your mama would be ashamed of!"

Jonathan listened to what Anton was saying, and his words, as mocking as they were, cut through him like a knife. Jonathan lost control and balled up his fist. With all his might, he punched Anton across the jaw.

Anton, stunned and angry, grabbed Jonathan around the waist and wrestled him to the floor. Both men were throwing blows while Alex tried to stop them. At that moment, Mike and Frank came in. Mike was stunned to see Jonathan and Anton fighting and ran over and grabbed the two men. "You punk!" Anton yelled to the top of his voice. "If you put your hands on me again, I'll kill your ass!"

"You better leave Taylor alone. I'm not going to tell you again."
"Taylor doesn't want you. She's with me—get that through your head! Now get out of my shop!"

"I'll leave, but I'll be back!" Jonathan straightened out his clothes and headed for the door with Alex close behind.

"Asshole!" Anton yelled.

"Punk bastard!" yelled Jonathan. He got in his SUV, Alex got into the passenger's seat, and they drove down First Avenue.

"If you wouldn't have stopped me, I would have killed that bastard!" Jonathan yelled as he stepped on the gas.

"Slow down! You're going to get us killed!" Alex yelled.

Jonathan slowed down, drove to the curve, and pulled over. He lowered his head, took a deep breath, and began to calm down. "You think Taylor did what Anton said she did last night?" Jonathan asked.

"No. Anton's an asshole. Taylor is a good person, and she wouldn't give it up that easy. Don't let him get to you. Just talk to Taylor tomorrow and try to get her to see Anton for what he really is. Taylor is the kind of person who sees the good in people. She could be easily deceived," Alex said.

Jonathan listened to what Alex was saying. Then he started the engine and drove slowly down the street. "You want to go to Roscoe's?" Jonathan asked.

"Sure," Alex said. "Hey, they are opening a new batting cage and a miniature golf. When it opens, we could go and check it out." Alex tried his best to get Jonathan's mind off Taylor.

"Yeah. We should do that."

Back at the shop, Anton walked over to the mirror and looked at his face. There were no marks, but his jaw still stung from Jonathan's blow.

"That bastard … I'll kill him," he said to Mike who was standing behind him.

"What happened?" Mike asked.

"Those two silly punks came into the shop and began to make demands. I knew when I saw him looking at me and Taylor at the diner the other day that he was interested in Taylor. He's just salty that Taylor is with me. Why is everyone in this town so against me and Taylor? Is Taylor some kind of goddess or something?"

"Well, people know how you are, Anton," Mike said. "What do you mean *how I am*?"

"You know what I mean. They know you've been in and out of trouble since high school, and they know Taylor is a good person. And you don't mean Taylor any good—you said it yourself," Mike said, looking at Anton.

Anton looked down as Mike spoke, and Mike saw the expression on his face.

"You're beginning to have feelings for Taylor," Mike said.

Anton walked into the backroom. "What if I am?" he asked.

Mike smiled. "There's nothing wrong with that. You just have to get past the sheriff."

"And Jonathan," Frank added.

"I didn't want to hurt that punk, but if he comes in my face again, I'm going to kill him. As for the sheriff, Taylor is a grown person. She makes her own decisions; besides, he can't put me in jail."

"But he can make things hard for you, Anton," Mike pointed out. "You don't want that; besides, I have a guy coming here in an hour. I want you to meet him. He was telling me something I think you and Frank are going to be interested in." "What is it?" Frank asked.

"I can't say until he comes, but it's going to be very interesting."

"Well, you better make it fast, because I have to meet Taylor tonight," Anton said.

"You are really falling for her. You have been with her every night this week," Mike said.

"Anton is in love," Frank teased.

"Shut up, Frank," Anton said. "It's just that Taylor is a sweet person. She's not like those other girls at Leo's. I can actually talk to her."

Chapter 17

ANTON FINISHED WASHING Mr. Holmes's car. He had changed the oil and rotated the tires. He looked at the clock and saw it was five o'clock, so he began to close up. He lowered the garage door and walked around to the front where he closed the door to the shop and turned on the closed sign. He then swept and tidied up the place. Mike and Frank were waiting in the break room when Anton came in.

"Where is this guy? It's five thirty," Anton asked. "He'll be here soon," Mike said.

"What does he want?"

"I can't say right now. Let him tell you. Just have an open mind and listen to what he has to say."

"He better make it quick. I have to go meet Taylor." "Where are you guys going tonight?" Frank asked.

"I don't know. I think I might take her to Roscoe's or Club 57," Anton said. "I'm not sure."

"Take her to Club 57. She would like that place. I took Ashley there for her birthday, and we had a ball. You would get out of town for a little while, and maybe you'll get lucky," Frank said.

"I want to show Taylor a good time. I don't want to do anything that's going to make her uncomfortable," Anton said.

"Look at you. Taylor must have really done something to you," Mike said, laughing.

"No. It's just that I want to do things right for once," Anton said.

Just then, someone knocked on the shop door.

"That's him," Mike said, excited.

Anton walked over and opened the door. A tall, lean man with dark, curly hair and a goatee stood at the door. "Hi. You must be Anton," he said, smiling as he reached out to shake Anton's hand.

"I am," Anton said. "Come in."

The man walked in and looked around.

"James," Mike said as he walked up to the man and gave him a hug. "This is Frank," he added, introducing his friend.

James shook Frank's hand. "You met Anton," Mike added. "Yes, I did."

"Well, let's get started," Mike said.

The men walked to the break room, and Anton motioned for James to sit down. They all sat around the break room table.

"Did Mike tell you anything about why I'm here?" James asked Anton. "No. He said that he was going to let you tell me," Anton said.

"Okay. Well, first of all, my name is James, and I work for Dunbar Armored Truck Company. Me, Mike, and a couple of guys I work with came up with a plan to make some cash—fast and easy. It's a foolproof plan, and if we do it right, no one will get hurt."

Anton looked at James and then Mike, who had all his attention on James. "What is this foolproof plan?" Anton asked, curious.

"Every third Thursday of the month, our company transports $20 million in cash to the First National Bank of Austin. It takes the same route every trip at the same time. My friends Bill and Jose are assigned to that route, and we came up with a plan that we could fake a robbery, take the money, and ensure no one gets hurt," James explained.

"What do you mean fake a robbery?" Anton asked, feeling unsure about the plan.

"Well," James said, "when the truck pulls up to the back of the bank, one guard gets out, and one guard stays in the truck. That's when you guys come in. You come in with guns, and rob Bill and José. Exchange some gunfire, José will give you the cash, and you drive off. Wear masks so you won't get recognized. After it's all over and the police stop investigating, we split the money six ways."

"It sounds easy," Anton said, "but how are you going to convince people that this was an actual robbery?"

"We thought of that too," Mike said. "Maybe if you shoot Bill or José in the leg, not fatally wounding him, it would be believable."

"I don't know. What if we get caught? We will go to jail for a long time, and I don't want to go back to jail," Anton said.

"It's a foolproof plan. No one will go to jail," Mike said.

"I don't know … I'll have to think about it," Anton said as he got up and walked to the front of the shop.

James looked at Mike. "I thought you said he'd be on board," he said. "I thought so. I have to talk to him some more," Mike said.

"I'm on board," Frank said. "I think it's a good idea."

"Let me talk to Anton some more," Mike said. "I know I can convince him. He's my buddy … He will come around."

"Okay," James said. "I don't want anyone to screw this up." "He won't. He'll come around," Mike said.

James got up and walked to the front of the shop. Anton was standing behind the counter.

"Think about it, man. I'm sure you could use the money," James said. "I'll think about it," Anton said. He smiled as he shook James's hand. James then hugged Mike and stepped out the door. Anton closed the door behind him.

"What do you think, Anton?" Mike asked.

"I don't know. I don't think that it's going to be that easy. If we rob the bank, that means the FBI is going to be involved. We could get in a lot of trouble. I already have a record, and I don't want to get in any more trouble. I'm not saying you couldn't do it, Mike. If you feel you want to take that risk, then go ahead."

"You know I don't want to do it without you," Mike said.

"Let me think about it," Anton said. "It's 6:15. I have to go." He gathered his stuff and turned off the lights.

Anton, Mike, and Frank locked up before leaving the shop.

Anton got in his car feeling insulted that Mike would try to get him involved in such a scam. Mike was always the kind of person who would lead someone else into trouble but never really get into trouble himself.

It was Mike's idea to rob the liquor store. He talked Anton into doing it, and Anton was the only one who paid for it—with three years of his life.

Three years is a piece of cake compared to what they might get if they tried to pull off this new job. *No,* Anton thought. *This time I'm not going to be the scapegoat. I'm not that stupid.* He picked up his phone and texted Taylor: "I'm running late." Then he started his engine and began driving toward the diner. *Mike can do this on his own. He doesn't need me. I'm not going back to jail for anyone*, he thought to himself.

Anton walked into the diner and saw Taylor talking to Maria at the counter while she waited for him to arrive.

"Hey, baby," he said as he leaned over to kiss her on the cheek.

Maria walked over to the window and picked up Mrs. Wilson's plate. "Are you guys going to eat here?" she asked.

"Do you want to, Taylor? I thought we could go to Austin for a while," Anton said.

"Okay," Taylor said, excited.

Anton looked at Taylor and thought about the future they could have together. But they wouldn't have that future if he was caught robbing an armored truck.

"Anton!" Taylor called. "You seem a million miles away." "I'm sorry, Taylor. I have something on my mind."

"Do you care to talk about it?"

"No. It's nothing really. I just have to talk to Mike and get something off my chest. Don't worry about it ... I's not about you."

"Okay," Taylor said. "Do you want to go to Roscoe's? I have never been there."

"Sure, Taylor. If you want, we could go to Roscoe's."

Taylor stood up and gathered her things before following Anton out to his car. Anton held tightly to her hand as they walked down Main Street. The sun was just beginning to set as the sky turned a dark purple. A cool breeze blew against Taylor's cheek. She shivered a little and grabbed her jacket to close it up around her neck. She looked at Anton and noticed his thoughts seemed to be occupied. She wondered what was so heavy on his mind, but she was too afraid to ask.

Chapter 18

THE SHOPPING MALL was busy with people was walking shoulder to shoulder, carrying bags as they laughed and talked. Taylor and Zoe walked through the mall, looking into the glass windows at the merchandise displayed there. It was the end of October, and the mall was already decorated for Christmas. There was a gigantic Christmas tree in the center of the mall, and they already had a place picked out for the shopping mall's Santa.

Little children were excited and happy as they rode in the old fashioned electric train that took them around the mall. Zoe and Taylor took the escalator up to the second floor where the food court was. They stopped and looked in the window of A to Z Electronics. The window displayed a sixty-five-inch, curved high-definition television—one of the biggest Taylor had ever seen. The color was so clear that Taylor could see every little mark on the news anchor's face. She had a high definition television at home, but the color on this television was ten times better.

"Technology is always improving," Taylor said to Zoe.

"Yes, one day what you buy is new, and the next day it's an antique," Zoe said.

They looked through the window at the new Macs and PCs.

"I have to get a new computer," Zoe said. "My old one is running too slow." Just then, a young man walked up to Zoe. He was an employee in the electronics shop. "You said you need a new computer? We have just what you need. Are you a Mac or a PC person?

Zoe looked at Taylor. "I was just looking … I'm not ready to buy a computer right now," she said.

"Why? Don't you have the money? You can apply for our easy line of credit—zero down and no payment till February."

"That sounds good," Zoe said, "but not today."

"Come on … You look like a student. I know you need that new computer. Just come with me and look around." Zoe and Taylor followed him into the store.

"Now, we have HP, Mac, Toshiba … You name it, we have it. So, are you a Mac or a PC person?"

Zoe laughed and said, "I'm a PC person." Zoe looked at the young man and felt her heart flutter. He was tall and had a medium build. His hair was auburn, and had a beard—Zoe was a sucker for a man with a beard.

"A PC … We have just the thing: an HP PC. It's on sale; plus, you get 10 percent off if you apply for our line of credit. Oh, by the way, my name is Todd."

Todd ushered Zoe over to the counter where she filled out an application for the credit, and to her amazement, she was approved. Then Todd preceded with checkout process.

"Do you need a printer? Virus protection?" Todd asked.

"No," Zoe said. "This is all I need." She usually didn't give in so easily, but Todd was so cute she couldn't resist.

Taylor and Zoe hurried out of the door and walked down to the food court. "What do you feel like today?" Taylor said.

"I don't know … Let's get Chinese." "Okay," Taylor agreed.

The friends walked over to Yellow Dragon and began to order. Taylor could smell the onions and chicken cooking on the grill behind the counter. She ordered pepper steak, and Zoe ordered orange chicken. Then they found a table and sat down.

"After we eat, I want to go to the Gap and get those blue jeans I was telling you about," Taylor said. "They will look nice with my gold blouse." Zoe nodded as she ate her orange chicken. She was thinking about how she could persuade Taylor to go out with Jonathan. She didn't want to upset Taylor, but she felt that Jonathan would make a great companion for Taylor, and he'd been a good friend since the third grade.

She looked at Taylor, who was going on and on about the gold blouse that she'd bought in Austin last week. Finally, Zoe decided to just come out with it and tell her how she felt—let her know that Jonathan was really interested, and Anton was scum and meant her no good.

Zoe thought again about what Jonathan had told her on Monday before she began.

"Taylor," Zoe said, interrupting her. "Yes?" Taylor said.

"You know, Jonathan has a new SUV." "I know. I saw it the other day."

"You know, he really likes you. He's wanted to ask you out for some time now," Zoe said.

"I know ... I could sense it. I like Jonathan—I do—but Anton has already asked me out. We are dating," Taylor said.

Zoe looked at Taylor and could see she was serious about Anton. "Taylor, Anton is a player. Do you really think he's serious about you?" "Yes," Taylor said. "He tells me every day."

"Taylor, how many girls have you seen Anton with in the past two months?" Zoe asked.

"Before me, a lot. But he hasn't been with anyone else since we've been together," Taylor insisted.

Zoe listened to what Taylor had to say and then thought about what Jonathan and Alex had told her about the redheaded girl. "Are you sure about that?" Zoe asked.

"I know," Taylor said. "Why can't people just accept the fact that Anton and I are dating, and I'm not interested in anyone else?" She was frustrated and began tapping her finger on the table.

"I just think you should see other people before you make up your mind about Anton," Zoe explained. "You hadn't been dating anyone at all before Anton, and I don't think you should just settle for him. Why don't you go out with Jonathan and see what he's like before you make up your mind and settle for Anton?"

Taylor thought about what Zoe was saying. She liked Jonathan too—he was tall and handsome, and he had a lot going for him. Plus, her father really liked him. Maybe she should give him a shot ... but then she saw Anton in her mind, and her heart flipped, and a tingling sensation went through her body. She thought about all the years she waited for this moment, and she couldn't think of anyone else but Anton.

"I'm sorry, Zoe. I know you mean well, but I guess I love Anton."

Zoe jumped when she heard Taylor use the word *love*. "But, Taylor, you've only been going out with him for two weeks."

"But I've loved him all of my life. Those two weeks feel like two decades. Anton and I talk about everything. We have so much in common—we like the same movies, music, and books."

"The same books?" Zoe said

"Yes, the same books. Anton reads books. He is a very intelligent person. He just had some bad breaks, but he's getting his life together."

Zoe wanted to tell Taylor about what Jonathan had said, but she wanted Jonathan to tell her himself—after all, he had the video. Besides, Zoe figured that no matter what she said, Taylor was never going to come around.

"What about your father?" she finally had to ask.

"My father's is still upset, but he'll come around when he sees that Anton isn't going to hurt me," Taylor said. "Do you want to go look at those pants now?"

"Sure," Zoe answered.

They got up and walked to the Gap, and Taylor showed Zoe the stonewashed straight-leg jeans she had been talking about.

"I bet Anton would love me in these," Taylor said as she held them up in front of her.

"Jonathan would love them too," Zoe said.

Taylor heard what Zoe said, but she didn't comment. She didn't want to lose Zoe's friendship, but she couldn't understand why her friend—her best friend—was so against her boyfriend. The whole town, it seemed, was against Anton, and Taylor thought that was unfair. She wished that she and Anton could leave town and never come back. All she heard all day from her father was what kind of person Anton was, and now she had to hear it from her friend.

"You want to try the pants on, Taylor?" Zoe asked.

"Yes, I'll be right back." Taylor stepped into the dressing room and tried on the pants. They hugged her hips and thighs the way she wanted. "Anton will really like me in these," she said as she took them off. She folded them before stepping back out of the dressing room. Taylor then went up to the checkout and bought the pants.

"Do you want anything else before we go?" Taylor asked Zoe. "I want a giant pretzel and a Coke."

Taylor laughed as they made their way to the pretzel stand.

Chapter 19

IT WAS THE seventh day in two weeks that the weather had been in the nineties. The sun was exploding with heat. The sidewalk was so hot it melted the soles of your shoes. There was little to no breeze, and stepping outside felt like stepping into a furnace.

Sheriff Murphy left his office early and ran to his car. He hurried and got inside—out of the inferno that had taken over the town. He drove to the grocery store and sat in the car for a while before tackling the heat again. He turned on the radio and heard the weatherman say the temperature was going to reach ninety-eight. The air-conditioning in the car was turned up to full force. The sheriff looked out over the parking lot and started to open the car door, but he hesitated because he didn't want to go out into the heat.

A car drove past and blew its horn. The sheriff looked and saw Mr. Wilson waving as he drove by. The sheriff sat up and gathered his things and then stepped out of the car and into the heat that awaited him in the parking lot.

He pressed the door lock and walked toward the store. He noticed that a new kid was gathering the grocery carts instead of Jonathan. He was a short kid, about fourteen years of age. The sheriff had never seen him around town before.

He walked into the store, and Mr. Rodriguez, the store manager, walked up to him. "Sheriff, I am glad you are here. I just hired a new night watchman I'd like you to meet. His name is Al. He's not here right now, but he will be in an hour."

"Oh … What happened to Bob, your last night guy?" the sheriff asked.

"Bob found another job in Austin. He and his family moved last week. We have been interviewing for the past week now. We finally decided on Al. He used to be a security guard for First National Bank in Austin."

"I see," the sheriff said. "When he has time, send him to my office, and I will talk to him."

"Yes, Sheriff," Mr. Rodriguez said.

"I see you have a new kid working in the parking lot," the sheriff noted.

"What happened to Jonathan?"

"Oh, that's Tim Armstrong. He just moved here about three weeks ago with his parents. We hired him part time to help Jonathan. Jonathan has been busy at school lately, and Tim is only helping until Jonathan comes back. Tim is a good kid. I'm surprised you haven't met him yet."

"No, I heard about the Armstrongs, but I haven't gotten around to introducing myself yet. I've been busy trying to keep things in order around town. You know, Halloween is coming up, and I have a town full of teenage practical jokers—and not just the teenagers, but the older kids as well. I can't wait until November when all of this Halloween business is over."

The sheriff grabbed a cart. "I'll see you later, Mr. Rodriguez." "I'll see you, Sheriff."

The sheriff walked down the potato chip aisle and began looking for his favorite chips. The Houston Astros were in the playoffs, and he, Deputy Mark, and Deputy Tom were going to watch the game on television. The Astros had been doing great this year—maybe this could be their year. He grabbed a couple of bags of Doritos and a large bag of potato chips before heading to the cookie aisle.

He was a sucker for Oreos. He and Taylor loved Oreos. They had been his favorite ever since he was a little boy. He couldn't go a day without them. Every time he ran out, he had to go to the store to buy more. He put two bags in his cart and looked at the Chips Ahoy cookies. They were sitting next to the Oreos. *I think I get a bag of these*, he silently decided.

The sheriff placed the cookies in his cart and then turned around. Spotting the dip for the potato chips, he decided to get some of that as well. He walked over and read the different flavors before settling on French onion and ranch.

He looked over the items in his cart and decided to buy some soda for Taylor and a case of beer for himself and the deputies. He started for the beverage aisle. When he heard laughter coming from the aisle next to him, he looked over and saw it was Mrs. Smith.

"You know, Linda, I thought Taylor was a good girl. Her father brags on her like she's a saint," Mrs. Smith said to Mrs. Johnson, one of the town gossipers.

The sheriff's heart dropped as he stood there listening to Mrs. Smith. "I know you see how she dresses now. She dresses like the town slut," Mrs. Johnson pointed out.

The sheriff began to crack his knuckles and clenched his teeth. He looked through the space of the shelves at Mrs. Smith and Mrs. Johnson as they continued.

"You know she didn't dress like that until she started going out with that no-good Anton," Mrs. Smith said.

"How could her father, who's supposed to be the town's sheriff, allow her to go out with him?" Mrs. Johnson said.

"I don't think he allows her to. I've heard them arguing about it on many occasions. Taylor just does what she wants to do," Mrs. Smith said. "How can he keep order in the town if he can't keep his own daughter in line?" Mrs. Johnson said.

The sheriff began to shake as a violent sensation fell over him. He shifted from foot to foot and held his breath.

"You know, Taylor comes home at all times of night. She's out at that Leo's until the break of day. She doesn't spend time with Zoe too much anymore either. She hangs out with those whores Tammy and Ashley," Mrs. Smith said.

The sheriff listened as Mrs. Smith spoke. He thought back to when he told Taylor that she was going to be the talk of the town, but she couldn't stop until it happened. Now she was—everyone was laughing and talking about how Anton was making a fool of her. *I won't stand for it*, he thought. *And how could Mrs. Johnson question my ability to handle my job? This town has been one of the safest places to live in Texas since I've been sheriff, and as for Taylor, I just haven't put my foot down. There are going to be some changes starting today.*

"You know, Taylor almost got laid off from her job because she couldn't make it in on time, and Anton would go to her job and hang out in the waiting room until she got off work. She got a warning from her supervisor," Mrs. Smith said. "The sheriff is going to have to do something. Anton is going to ruin that girl's whole life."

"It's a shame. I hate to see that happen. Taylor is a sweet girl," Mrs. Johnson said.

"Yes, until her mother died … Now the sheriff can't do a thing with her," Mrs. Smith noted.

Tears rolled down the sheriff's cheeks as he thought about his wife, Mary. *What would she say about all this? How would she handle Taylor? Tell me something, Mary. Give me a sign*, he thought as he wiped away his tears. "You know, the sheriff is really angry with Taylor. I hear that he is going to kick her out," Mrs. Smith said.

"Out the house?" Mrs. Johnson asked, surprised. "Yes."

"And where is she going to go? Poor thing. She'll probably end up with Anton until he gets tired of her. I pray she gets herself together before the sheriff has to come to that," Mrs. Johnson said.

The sheriff tightened up his lip, grabbed his cart, and pushed it over to the other side of the aisle.

"Sheriff," Mrs. Johnson said, surprise, "what brings you to the store?" She looked at his cart. "Looks like you're going to have a party."

"No. Tom, Mark, and I are going to watch the baseball playoffs."

"Oh, I see. Well, I was buying some ingredients to make a German chocolate cake," Mrs. Johnson said. "I'll send you a slice at the sheriff's office."

"That would be fine," he said, forcing a smile.

"I better get going. Walter is waiting for his dinner." She turned to leave, pushing her cart to the front of the store.

"I better get going too, Sheriff. I came to get some cat food. I'll see you around," Mrs. Smith said as she pushed her cart to the front of the store also.

The sheriff was furious. He wanted to scream, but instead, he composed himself and finished his shopping.

Chapter 20

"DO YOU SEE how she dresses now?" Those words rang in the sheriff's mind all day as he tried to work to take his mind off Mrs. Smith. "She looks like a slut." The sheriff tossed the words over and over in his mind. "Murphy! Murphy!" Deputy Tom called.

"What?" the sheriff answered, coming back to himself.

"You seemed like you were a million miles away," Tom said, laughing. "I'm sorry, Tom. What did you say?"

"I said Chris Sale is pitching tonight. The Astros are going to have a hard time."

"It doesn't matter. We have Justin Verlander. We are going to give the Red Sox a run for their money," Sheriff Murphy said as he drove down Main Street.

The deputy was looking into the stores as the car drove slowly down the street. "I like days like this when there is little to no excitement."

"Yeah, it seems like everyone is doing fine. We haven't had any major calls, and the businesses are doing great. If every day was like today, it would put the sheriff's department out of business," Murphy said.

"All units, there is a four-five-nine at 111 and Pine," Gloria announced. The sheriff jumped and looked at Tom. "A four-five-nine … That's Mrs. Scott's place," the sheriff said as he stepped on the gas and turned on his siren. The sheriff arrived at the house at the same time as deputies Mark and Jerry.

They got out of their cars and headed up the brick walkway of a gray stone bungalow with a big picture window. The door was closed, and the whole neighborhood was quiet.

"It looks quiet," the sheriff said as he looked around the yard. He noticed the grass was neatly cut, and the flower pots sitting by the door were untouched. He walked around the back to the patio and saw an empty lawn furniture set.

Next, he walked over to the garage and checked the door, but it was locked. He walked back up the front and met Tom and the other deputies at the door.

"Everything looks quiet," he repeated as he rang the doorbell. Mrs. Scott looked out the window before opening the door.

"Oh, Sheriff, I'm glad you're here," she said. Her hand was shaking, and her jaw was tight as she pressed her lips together. She wore a blue housecoat and a pair of blue house slippers. She held her collar closed with her left hand and waved the sheriff in with her right.

"There is someone in my house, Sheriff," Mrs. Scott said, shaking all over. "I could hear them. It sounds like they are in the walls."

"The walls?" Sheriff Murphy repeated back and as he looked at Mrs. Scott. "We'll get to the bottom of this. You stand out here with Deputy Jerry, while Mark, Tom, and I check things out."

The three men walked into the house and looked around. Every light in the house was on, and the television was on, but the sound was turned down. The sheriff looked around the living room. The couch looked as though it was from the late seventies and was covered with a plastic cover. The outdated green shag carpet had a long, plastic runner going across the living room and into the dining room. There were hardwood floors in the dining room, and the long dining room table sat neatly in the middle of the room.

"Do you hear that, Sheriff?" Mark asked as he stood in place in the dining room.

The sheriff listened and heard a low thumping sound that sounded like it was coming from the walls.

"What's that? Squirrels?" the sheriff said as he stuck his ear up to the wall. "I don't know," Tom said. "It sounds like it's coming from the attic."

They walked slowly up the stairs and looked up at the attic door. The sheriff pulled down the Staircase, and one by one, they went into the attic. It was dark and dusty, and the sheriff walked across the floorboards, carefully searching for the light bulb string in the middle of the attic ceiling. Cobwebs hung from the wooden beams on the ceiling, and the floor was filed with old boxes and trunks.

With the light on, they looked around but couldn't find the thumping sound, which grew faint when they reached the attic. The sheriff looked around one last time before he headed back down the stairs. As soon as he stepped foot on the floor, the thumping came back.

"I don't understand it," he said. "It's not in the attic." He checked every room on the second floor, but there was no person or thing that could be making the sound.

"Maybe it's an old pipe," Mark said as he looked under the bathroom sink at the elbow pipe.

"It could be a pipe of some kind," the sheriff said, tapping on the pipe. "Let's check out the kitchen. It could be her garbage disposal."

The sheriff and the deputies walked down the stairs and went into the kitchen. Deputy Tom opened the cabinets under the sink and tapped on the pipe, but there was no sound. The sheriff looked in the pantry and tapped on the pipe that was in the corner going up the wall, but there was no sound. He looked in the refrigerator and then in the stove, but he could not find the source of the sound.

He pressed his lips together and held his hands behind his back. "Let's check out the basement," he said, talking through clenched teeth. The men walked over to the basement door and opened it slowly.

The thumping grew louder as they descended into the basement. Deputy Tom found the light switch and turned it on. It was cool and dusty in the unfinished basement, and a crack snaked across the cold concrete floor. The electric panel box was closed on the far-right wall.

The sheriff looked up at the wooden beams on the ceiling and touched the pipe, but there was no sound.

There was another room closed off from the basement with a wooden door and drywall. The sheriff opened the door, and in the corner of the room was an old freezer whose motor was running and shaking the freezer from side to side, making a thumping sound. Tom ran over and reached behind the freezer to unplug it from the wall socket. The sheriff inhaled and exhaled. His pulse slowed down, and he smiled.

"It was the freezer," Tom said as he glanced at the sheriff.

"It was really making a fuss," the sheriff said as he patted Tom on the back. "There was no burglary, no home invasion, just a freezer."

They looked inside the freezer and discovered it was empty. Tom closed the door. They went upstairs and walked to the door to find Mrs. Scott.

"It's fine, Mrs. Scott. There is no one in your house. It was your old freezer in the basement that made that thumping sound," the sheriff said. "Oh, Sheriff, really? I'm glad you found the sound. It's scary being old and living alone."

"I know, Mrs. Scott, but there is nothing to worry about. If you need anything, just give me a call," the sheriff said with a smile.

"Thank you, Sheriff," Mrs. Scott said as she went into the house.

The sheriff and Tom got back into their squad car, and Mark and Jerry did the same.

"I'll see you two at the station," the sheriff said as he drove away. He drove, silently thinking about Mrs. Scott and the nasty freezer. Then Mrs. Smith crept back into his mind.

"She looked like a slut." He clenched his teeth and gripped the steering wheel. "You know, Sheriff, I don't want to pry, but is Taylor still seeing Anton?" Tom asked carefully.

The sheriff nodded yes as he kept his eyes on the road.

"I saw Anton the other day. He was with some redheaded girl. I was with some buddies I went to school with. They live in Austin, and we were at a bar and grill called Roscoe's. All the young people hang out there. I saw Anton hooked up with some redheaded girl. I thought I might tell you so that you can tell Taylor," Tom said.

"Taylor isn't listening to me these days," the sheriff said sadly.

"Well, then tell Anton to stay the hell away from your daughter, sir," Tom said.

"You know what I should do?" Murphy said. "I should catch him alone, kick his ass, drive him out of town, and dare him to come back."

"Yeah, you should do that, Sheriff. I will help you. Just let Anton get out of line with me ... I'll kill him. I know that was him and Mike who threw that chair off the balcony at the high school that hit my cousin Anthony Foley on the head. He was in a coma for two weeks, and when he woke up, he had to go to rehabilitation. That chair gave him fifteen stitches. So, yeah, I want to get that son of a bitch Anton and Mike. Let's do it."

"We'll do it this weekend. We have to catch him alone," the sheriff said. "We don't want him to cry police brutality."

"After him, let's get that Mike and that flunky Frank."

The sheriff drove down Main Street, visualizing what he was going to do to Anton and how he was going to stop Taylor from seeing him once and for all.

No, Son, this town isn't big enough for the both of us. One of us has to go, and it won't be me, he thought as he gripped the steering wheel and smiled.

Chapter 21

MR. BOOKSTIEN, TAYLOR'S biology teacher, was showing slides of the three basics shapes of bacteria. Taylor was fidgeting around in her seat as her eyes slowly drooped, and she could feel herself drifting away. She jumped up and began taking notes to keep herself awake. She squinted at the images on the screen, but all she could see was little dots moving around in a circle.

She had been working thirteen hours a day three days a week, trying to tackle a sixteen-credit-hour course load, and seeing Anton. She had to take a break. She didn't want her schoolwork to suffer because she had a boyfriend, but her father really laid it on thick when he suddenly told her that he wasn't going to pay her tuition next semester.

Since then, she had been working every chance she got, so she could cover the cost. Now her sleep time was suffering, but she did not want to beg her father for anything. She wanted to show him she could do it. Although she had been working a lot, her grades hadn't suffered yet. She got a B on her last biology test, and she managed to make her clinicals.

If she could make it through midterms, she would be all right. *Just a couple more weeks*, she thought.

She looked up at Zoe, who seemed to be in the swing of things as she looked at the board and took notes. She then looked at Jonathan, whose eyes she met as he looked at her from across the room. He smiled.

Taylor looked down at her book.

Jonathan took out his phone and texted her. "Can we talk?"

Taylor looked at her phone and then at Jonathan. "When?" she texted. "After class," he texted back.

"Sure."

Mr. Bookstien looked at Taylor, who hid her phone in her book bag. *I wonder what Jonathan wants*, she thought. Then she thought about what Zoe had said the other day. Fear came over her, and she began to shake. She liked Jonathan as a friend, but she didn't want to take it any further than that.

She had Anton, and Anton was taking all her time. Suddenly, Taylor was wide awake. The anticipation of talking to Jonathan overwhelmed her. She didn't want to hurt his feelings and lose his friendship, and she didn't want to lead him on. She sunk down in her seat and watched the slides and listened to Mr. Bookstien's monotone voice as it filled the classroom, putting everyone to sleep.

The lesson on bacteria that week wasn't too exciting. Taylor had a hard time focusing in class, and she didn't comprehend much in her reading either. She wasn't looking forward to next week's test, as she knew she wasn't prepared.

Mr. Bookstien finally turned off the slide projector and began handing out the study guide for next week's test. Taylor got her sheet, looked over it, and stuck it in her book bag. Zoe, Jonathan, and Alex were talking over by Jonathan's seat. The other students hurried out of class as soon as Mr. Bookstien dismissed them.

Taylor walked over to Jonathan and Zoe. Jonathan motioned for her to take a seat. Mr. Bookstien was gathering his things, and Jonathan waited for him to leave.

"I'll see you kids next week," he said as he headed for the door. Jonathan smiled at Taylor, and Alex and Zoe walked over to the window to give them some privacy. Taylor's heart began to pound, and her palms felt sweaty as she waited for Jonathan to speak.

A lump grew in Jonathan's throat, and his heart felt as if it were going to jump out of his chest. He wanted to talk to Taylor and tell her everything that had been going on. He wanted to save her from that bastard Anton, but he was scared of being rejected. He knew Taylor liked Anton more than she liked him when he saw Taylor with Anton that night at the diner. He knew that he'd lost all hope of being with her, so he was scared to tell her what he wanted to say. He didn't want to lose her twice.

He looked at Alex, and Alex waved and whispered, "Tell her, man." Jonathan took a deep breath and exhaled. "Taylor, I have something to tell you about Anton that I think you should know."

Taylor looked at Jonathan and rolled her eyes. *You too?* she thought. Jonathan began to tremble when he saw the look on Taylor's face.

Then he pulled out his phone with the video he was going to use to back up his story.

"Last week Alex and I went to Roscoe's in Austin—you know, the place everyone has been talking about." "I know Roscoe's," Taylor said.

"Well, we were hanging out, and we saw Anton there."

"I know Anton went to Roscoe's the other day," Taylor said, interrupting. "He told me."

"Well did he tell you he was with another girl?" Jonathan said. Taylor's eyes widened, and she looked at Jonathan. *He's lying*, she thought. *He just wants me to be angry at Anton.*

"Another girl?" she said.

"Yes, another girl," Jonathan said, trying to read Taylor's expression. "He was hugging up with a girl and kissing all over her. He paid for her dinner and all of her drinks."

Taylor looked wide-eyed at Jonathan. and her heart sunk as she pressed her lips together. A numbing sensation moved over her.

"Why are you lying?!" she said in a low voice. "Why does everyone have to lie on Anton?"

"I'm not lying," Jonathan protested. "I have proof." He turned on the video and showed it to Taylor.

She looked at him and then hesitated and took the phone. The video showed Anton hugging a redheaded girl, kissing her, and laughing. Tears formed in Taylor's eyes, and a rage came over her.

There must be some kind of explanation, she thought. "What date is on this video?" she asked in disbelief, hoping that it was an old video.

Jonathan showed her the date that read October 15—exactly a week ago. "There must be some kind of explanation," she said to Jonathan.

"If he tells you anything other than he was dating that girl, he's lying," Jonathan said. "He was kissing that girl all night, and that was the weekend. He probably spent a night with her."

Taylor wanted to scream. Everything everybody was saying about Anton was right—her father, Zoe, and now Jonathan. She felt like a fool. She kept thinking that there must be some kind of explanation.

Anton seems so sweet. He can't be doing this to me, she thought. How was she going to face her father after what she'd said to him, and now it turned out that he was right? How was she going to face him?

She looked at Jonathan, who was looking at her to read her reaction.

"That's not all, Taylor. There's more."

Taylor looked down at the floor and then at Jonathan.

"Just this Friday at the bowling alley, Alex and I ran into Anton, Frank, and Mike. Anton was bragging about how he had you under his thumb."

Taylor's eyes widened as she bit her lip. "How he had me under his thumb?" "Yes," Jonathan answered. "That means—"

"I know what that means, Jonathan," Taylor snapped. "I'm not stupid." "I was just telling you."

"Well go on."

"He was calling you a stupid bitch and a whore."

A numbing filling rose in Taylor's chest as tears formed in her eyes. "He said all he wanted to do was score with you, and then he was going to drop you like a hot potato. Alex and I heard all of this. He was talking loudly and bragging and acting disrespectful. Tammy and Ashley were there too. They were calling you a fool. They talked about how you dress and how country you are.

"Taylor, Anton said that he would never be serious about a dweeb like you. They talked about your friends and how you think you are something because you live on the east end. Anton talked about your father too … He said that he hopes that someone either shoots your father or hurts him really badly, because he thinks he's so tough."

Taylor looked at Jonathan and straightened up her clothes. "Thank you for telling me this, Jonathan. I have to get to the bottom of this. Anton didn't give me any indication that he was out to harm me. I know Mike doesn't really care for me, and neither do Tammy and Ashley. But I thought Anton was different."

"Anton is an ass hole, Taylor," Jonathan said. "He's not a good person. All he does is walk all over people. He has no respect for people—not even the law." Jonathan felt bad for Taylor.

"I have to think about what I'm going to do," Taylor said. "I have to talk to Anton." She then got up and gathered her things.

Zoe walked over and rubbed her arm. "Are you okay?" she asked. "Yes," Taylor said, forcing a smile. "I'll be okay. I'm a big girl." "Do you want to talk?" Zoe asked.

"No. I have to get home. It looks like a storm is coming; besides, I have to cook dinner for my father."

"Be careful driving," Jonathan said. "It looks like it's getting bad outside." "Yes," Taylor said. "I better get going." She was hurt and embarrassed, and she felt like a fool. She walked out the door and ran down the hall, ducking into the bathroom where she began to cry. Her father was right. Anton was nothing but scum. How could she face her father or anyone else? She hit her chest, trying to rid herself of the stabbing pain in her heart, but it stabbed and stabbed at her, and she cried.

Chapter 22

TAYLOR WALKED OUT of the science building and made her way to the parking lot. The sky was turning dark gray from the storm. Clouds formed overhead, and the wind was high, blowing paper and other debris across the parking lot.

"I have to get home and out of the storm," Taylor said as she hurried to her car. She opened the door and stepped into the car. She turned on the windshield wipers, fastened her seat belt, and turned on the radio.

"A tornado watch is in effect for Blanco County," the voice on the radio said.

"A tornado?! I have to get home to the basement," Taylor said. As she drove out of the parking lot and down the street, she saw the image of the redheaded girl kissing Anton, and her pulse began to pound. She bit her lip, and tears rolled down her cheeks.

"How could he do this to me?" she said. "He acts so nice to me when he's around me. We have such a good time."

She thought about when they were at the park sitting under the stars and how gentle and caring Anton was. She could hear him tell her that he liked her and that he wanted her to be his girl.

"Was that all a lie?" Taylor said as she sobbed. "Did you say all of those things to me so you can score?" Her heart dropped, and it felt like she was going to have a heart attack. The tears blurred her vision, and the rain on the windshield blocked her view, causing her to miss the stop sign and drive right into the intersection.

Mr. Sanders, an older gentleman, was coming home from the barbershop where he'd just gotten a new haircut and a beard trim. He was on his way to the grocery store to pick up some items for dinner. He had lived in San Juan all his life and was thought to be an easygoing person. He'd known the sheriff for a long time, voted for him in the election, and was pleased with his performance.

He liked Taylor as well and thought she was a good kid. He drove down First and stopped at the stop sign, looking both ways before entering the intersection. That's when he saw Taylor speed through. He hit his brakes and turned to the side. Taylor saw Mr. Sanders as she went through the intersection. She stepped on her brakes and skidded to the side. Her heart leaped, and she felt as though she wanted to vomit.

She sat in the car, shocked by what had just happened. She thought about the accident she almost had, took a deep breath, and got out of the car. Mr. Sanders sat and stared at Taylor as he thought about what could have occurred. He had just bought his 2017 Ford Explorer, and he had a large car note. He gripped the steering wheel and clenched his teeth as his blood boiled over inside of him. Then he jumped out the car.

"Are you crazy?!" he yelled to the top of his voice. "You could have killed me!" he looked at his car and then shook his fist at Taylor. "All you kids do is speed down the street like you have nine lives! You didn't see the stop sign? Are you blind?"

Taylor was upset by what had just happened, and she was furious at Anton. She knew the incident was her fault, but anyone can make a mistake.

Rage rose up in her, and she ran up to Mr. Sanders and waved her finger in his face. "This could have happened to anyone. You should be glad we didn't have an accident!"

Mr. Sanders stepped back, and fire rose in him. "Who are you talking to like that, young lady? I'm old enough to be your father!"

"Well you are not my father. You don't talk to me any kind of way!" Taylor yelled.

"Watch where you're going. You need to learn how to drive!" yelled Mr. Sanders.

"I drive just fine," Taylor said.

"You get your hand out of my face … I don't know who you think you are!" Mr. Sanders yelled.

"You know who I am, and if you don't, I'm Taylor, asshole!" "No, you're a little bitch," Mr. Sanders said.

Taylor looked around and saw a crowd had gathered on the corner to watch her and Mr. Sanders argue. She became embarrassed, and her cheeks turned red as she thought about what her father might say.

"You young people think you own the world," Mr. Sanders said.

"Just get back into your car. I didn't hit you," Taylor protested. She then turned around and got back in her car.

Mr. Sanders climbed back into his car, mumbling to himself. "The nerve of some people. I never thought Taylor would talk back to me the way she did." He backed up, straightened out his car, looked at Taylor, and drove away.

Taylor started her engine and proceeded down the street. She couldn't get Anton out of her mind. The thought of him being with another woman drove her crazy.

The rain was coming down heavily. Taylor could hardly see the street as she drove, so she slowed down and turned on her brights.

"All he wants to do is score." She heard Jonathan's words over and over in her mind. Taylor felt like throwing up. A knot formed in her stomach, and a sour taste was in her mouth.

"Maybe Jonathan is right. Maybe I should forget about Anton," she said to herself as she cried. "Please stop crying, Taylor. At least you have friends who care enough to tell you what's going on. Maybe I should go to the concert with Jonathan and forget about Anton. He is a liar and a cheat, and I should never have trusted him."

Taylor finally pulled into the driveway and turned off the engine. She sat in the car for a few minutes and waited for the rain to die down.

She reached in her purse and pulled out her phone. Taylor looked at Zoe's number for a while and then dialed it. The phone rang twice before Zoe answered.

"Hello?" Zoe said. She had just made it to the diner and changed into her uniform when her phone rang.

"Hello, Zoe," Taylor said, sobbing.

"Oh my God ... Taylor, are you all right? Where are you?" Zoe asked

"I'm okay," Taylor said. "I'm sitting in front of my house waiting for the rain to stop." "Oh."

"I just wanted to talk," Taylor said.

"Sure. We can talk," Zoe said. "Let me go to the back." Zoe called for Maria to cover for her and then headed to the back room. She found a quiet place between the shelves in the stockroom. "We can talk now," Zoe said. "I was thinking about what Jonathan said. You were right about Anton, Zoe. I should have listened ... I'm such a fool."

"I'm sorry you had to hear it this way," Zoe said, "but it's better you find out now rather than later."

"Did you see the video Jonathan had? It's horrible."

"I saw it, Taylor, but that's how Anton, Mike, and Frank are. Anton doesn't know how to be faithful. He doesn't care about anyone but himself. He just wanted to use you to get back at the sheriff for arresting him—like it's your dad's fault. Anton is just one of those people who blames others for their problems."

"I really liked Anton too. I thought that was serious. He never let on he was playing me."

"That was the plan, Taylor. That's how he was reeling you in. He wanted you to fall in love with him so he could use you and dump you, and then he was going to spread it all over town."

Rage rose up in Taylor as she thought about what Zoe said. "Just wait till I see him. I'll show him what kind of person I can be. I'm not as dumb as he thinks. The nerve of him ... Who does he think he is? What hurts me, Zoe, is that my father was right about the wedge Anton tried to put between us." It was all in his plan. He wanted me and my father to have a falling out. All of those lies about how we were going to be together no matter what—how no one was going to stand in our way. They were all lies. I feel like such a fool."

Zoe listened as Taylor went on about Anton. She knew her friend was hurting, but she didn't know how to make it better. "Well, you know now, Taylor. Just go your separate ways and forget about Anton. I know Jonathan is still interested. You should call him tonight see what he has planned for the weekend."

"I'll do that. Thank you, Zoe."

"No problem, Taylor ... I better get back to work now. We'll talk soon." "Okay. Well ... bye," Taylor said.

"Bye," Zoe replied.

Chapter 23

THE WIND WAS howling when Taylor came in from school, and the rain was coming down hard. Taylor was soaked from the downpour. She took off her wet coat, shook her umbrella in the bathroom, and set it in the tub. She walked into the kitchen and turned on the lights, which began to flicker from the storm. Taylor looked out the window, and it looked like midnight when it was just three in the afternoon. She got her book bag and set her biology book on the kitchen island.

She began thumbing through the pages but could not concentrate on her homework. All Taylor could think about was what Jonathan had said earlier in biology.

Maybe he was right maybe Anton is a player, and all he wants is one thing. Anton is known for running with certain types of girls. What does he really want with me? she thought. *Jonathan is smart, he's nice, and his parents are friends with my father. Jonathan will have a college degree in May. Anton doesn't even have a high school diploma. Zoe says he has a bad temper, and he and Mike are known for beating up on women. That's what my father is concerned about ... Maybe Daddy is right.*

Taylor flipped through the pages of her biology book, trying to throw the conversation she'd had with Jonathan and Zoe out of her mind. The thunder rumbled, and she could hear the rain falling on the roof like rocks. She went to the coffee maker and made herself a fresh cup before sitting back at the island.

Anton is trying to change his life, she thought. *He told me at the park what he is going to do. People have to give people a chance. I know my father is concerned for me, but he doesn't think I can take care of myself.*

As for Jonathan, it's Anton I want. Anton is the one for me. He would not do anything to hurt me. I think his bad temper for women is a thing of the past. Taylor looked out the window at the downpour of rain. She then went to the refrigerator, took out a casserole she'd made the night before, and stuck it in the oven.

Jonathan will make another girl happy one day, but that girl won't be me. I love Anton for good or bad. Anton is the one for me. Taylor then took out a pen and notepad and began writing out her homework assignment. The lights flickered again, and she went to the hall closet to get some candles and matches and set them on the island.

"Just in case the lights go out," she said aloud.

Just then, the doorbell rang and frightened Taylor. "Who could be at the door on a day like this? I know it's not Jonathan, and Zoe would have called … Oh no! Did something happen to Daddy?"

Taylor ran to the door and peeked out the window. To her surprise, it was Anton standing there shivering in the rain. She opened the door, smiled, and motioned for Anton to come inside.

"You're soaked," she said as he stepped through the door.

"I had to see you," he said, running his hand through his wet hair. "What I need to say couldn't wait."

Taylor looked at him with affection and wonder. He had on a black biker jacket that was zipped up to the collar, a pair of blue jeans, and a pair of black combat boots. His hair was saturated from the rain.

"You can't stay long," Taylor warned as he walked farther into the living room.

"I know," He said as he looked deep into her eyes.

Taylor's heart jolted hard, and all she wanted to do was kiss him.

"I've been thinking seriously about us," he said. "I know your father doesn't approve of us, but it's not about your father. It's about you and me. I think I love you, Taylor. When I wake up in the morning, I think of you. When I go to bed at night, I dream of you. I've never felt this way about anyone else before."

"But Jonathan told me what you said at the bowling alley." Anton's eyes widened.

"He told me about how you called me names and how you said you wanted someone to shoot my father … And who was that redheaded girl?"

Anton stepped back. "I know I said a lot of things I didn't mean. I said those things because I wasn't serious at first, but now I am, and Amber is just a friend I met a while back in Austin. She doesn't mean a thing to me. I love you, Taylor."

Taylor's pulse pounded, and tears began to form in her eyes. She squinted to see Anton through the running tears. She started to speak, but a lump was in her throat, so she just smiled.

"I don't want to lose you," Anton continued.

"You're not going to lose me," Taylor managed to say.

"We are going to be together even if we have to leave this stinking town," Anton said. "I have some money saved up, and maybe we could go to Chicago. I have some family there, and I can get a job." "I have to finish school," Taylor said sadly.

"We can wait until you finish school. You are a big girl now. You don't need your father to finish school. You have to start doing things on your own," Anton said.

"I know, but I can't just leave my father like that. He'd never forgive me. I love my father, and I love you. I pray that we can work this out. My father isn't all that bad. He will come around ... We just have to give him a little time."

"Your father hates me," Anton said. "There is nothing you can say to him that will make him change his mind."

"You just have to trust me," Taylor said as she put her arm around Anton's neck.

He leaned down and kissed her, and Taylor's heart was swimming in heaven.

*****

Mrs. Smith was bringing her plants inside from the porch when she saw Anton go into the sheriff's house. She laughed, and her heart leaped as she looked over at the house.

"I knew Taylor was up to something when she came home early," she said to herself. "Going to sneak your boyfriend in while your daddy is a way? You can't get anything over on me ... I know everything that goes on in this town, missy."

Mrs. Smith stepped in from the rain and went to the kitchen where she pulled out a can of gourmet cat food from the top shelf of the pantry.

Then she opened it and put it in a white porcelain bowl.

"Here, girl," she called.

A yellow stripy cat with green eyes ran into the kitchen and began eating out of the white bowl.

"That's a girl," Mrs. Smith said as she rubbed the cat on the head. The woman then walked back to the window. The rain was coming down heavily, and there was no one on the street. She looked across at the sheriff's house and saw a shadow walk past the window. It was the large, shadowy figure of a man. Mrs. Smith knew it had to be Anton, but she could see no more than a shadow.

"I know Linda will want to know this," she said, smiling as she walked over to the end table and picked up her phone. She dialed Mrs. Johnson, who was at home fixing dinner for her husband.

"Linda, are you busy?" Mrs. Smith asked.

"Not really. I'm just finishing up Fred's dinner." "Well, I know you will want to hear this."

Mrs. Johnson checked the boiling pot on the stove, adjusted the fire, and went to sit down at her kitchen island. "Know what?" she asked.

"Anton is over at the sheriff's house, right as we speak. He's there with Taylor alone," Mrs. Smith said.

"What?" Mrs. Johnson said. "Do you think the sheriff knows?"

"You know the sheriff doesn't know. They could be doing God knows what—and under the sheriff's roof," Mrs. Smith said.

Ms. Johnson laughed. "Right under his nose. I thought Taylor was a better person than that. She seems so sweet."

"Well it's that Anton. He has her out at all times of the night. She dresses like a whore. Now he's sneaking over when the sheriff is not there. I wonder what's next," Mrs. Smith said.

"Tell me how long he stays," Mrs. Johnson said. "I've got to go finish up supper."

"Okay, Linda. Talk to you in a bit." Mrs. Smith hung up and walked back over to the window to peek out.

There was still no sign of anyone moving around. At the sheriff's house window there was a single yellow light, but that's all Mrs. Smith could make out through all the rain.

"I wonder what the sheriff would say about this," she said, laughing. The thunder roared, and the lightning flashed. Mrs. Smith went to her dining room table and turned on a battery-powered radio to listen to the weather report.

*****

Anton put on his coat and looked into Taylor's big brown eyes.

"I just don't want you to be hurt, Taylor. Your father can be a mean son of a bitch."

"He's not that way with me," Taylor said. Anton looked at her in disbelief.

"Really ... He's not. He wouldn't do anything to hurt me. I feel safe here." Anton walked to the window and looked outside. "You know, I've never been on this side of town before," he said as he looked at the houses on the other side of the street. "It seems strange being in the sheriff's house. If he knew, he would shoot me."

"I know. I seldom get visits from guys here," Taylor said. "It's not like I can't. I just don't. I wasn't interested at first."

"Well, you've got me now. You don't need anyone else," Anton said with a smile.

He looked around and then he walked to the door. "Give me one more kiss for the road." he said.

Taylor's knees buckled as she kissed him.

Anton opened the door and stepped out into the rain. He ran to his car and then turned and waved at Taylor as he ducked inside his car. Taylor waited until Anton drove off before she closed the door.

Mrs. Smith watched as Anton drove off. She then watched Taylor go inside and close the door.

Chapter 24

EDDIE FISHER WAS driving down Third Street really fast. His head was spinning, and his vision was blurred. He laughed uncontrollably as he passed a white SUV in the other lane. He drove right up to the back bumper of a minivan going the speed limit. Eddie honked his horn and tried to pass the van, but the van would not let him pass.

The traffic in the other lane was heavy, and Eddie couldn't cross over to the other lane. He honked again. "Move, bastard," he yelled as he stuck his hand out the window.

The van kept driving at a normal speed. Eddie's hand shook, and the car swirled from side to side and in and out of lanes.

"Come on," Eddie yelled, frustrated that the other car was moving too slow. He honked again, but the van kept driving at the same speed. Finally, the cars in the other lane moved up, and Eddie was able to switch lanes to where the cars were moving faster.

Eddie passed the van and stuck his middle finger up at the old lady who was driving in the van. The lady was appalled as she turned and looked at Eddie. Then he stepped on the gas and sped up, laughing uncontrollably. His eyes were blurred, and he could not see that the light had turned red. He sped through the intersection.

He sideswiped a Ford Focus, and the two cars were totally damaged. The Ford focus was totaled beyond recognition. Eddie was dazed as he sat in the driver's seat of his car, a 2016 Buick SUV. He tried to move, but a sharp pain traveled from his leg to his back. He touched his head and felt a wet stream of blood flowing from his forehead.

He began to slip in and out of consciousness. He looked over at the driver's side of the car he hit and saw a woman slumped over what used to be the steering wheel. On the ground a few feet from the wreckage was the body of a man lying facedown in a pool of blood.

People began to gather around, and an older gentleman called 911. Eddie felt sleepy, but his urge to laugh lingered even after he could no longer feel his legs.

Sheriff Murphy and Deputy Tom were driving down Main Street. The rain had stopped, and they were going to check out damages from the storm. When the call came in about the accident, the sheriff put on his siren and hurried to the scene. When he got there, he was shocked by how horrific the scene was. The man in the SUV was pinned between the steering wheel and the seat, and the woman in the Focus was mangled up among the debris from the car.

The fire department was already at the scene when the sheriff and Deputy Tom got there. "It's a mess," Fire Chief Logan said as he walked up to the sheriff. "We have two fatalities and this guy." Chief Logan pointed to Eddie. "You can smell the alcohol on him."

The firemen managed to get Eddie loose from the steering wheel. They laid him on a gurney to work on him, while the sheriff walked up to him and asked him his name.

"My name is Eddie, Eddie Fisher," he cried. "I'm sorry, Sheriff. I didn't see the light." He looked at the two bodies lying under sheets on the ground next to the wreckage. "Are they dead?" he cried. "I didn't mean to do it, Sheriff."

The sheriff took the driver's wallet from the paramedic and looked at his license. He was from Dallas. "What were you doing all the way out here?" the sheriff asked. He then walked over and looked under the sheet at the woman whose body was mangled, and his eyes widened because he recognized her. It was Sarah Turner, Mr. Turner's granddaughter. She was about Taylor's age and went to the university with Taylor and Jonathan. How was he going to tell his neighbor the news? This was the hard part of being a sheriff.

Deputy Tom helped put the bodies in the ambulance. He then walked over and began telling the people to move along. "All right, all right … It's over. Go home … There's nothing to see."

The tow truck moved the two mangled cars, and the ambulance took Eddie to the hospital.

The sheriff was quiet as he drove back to the office. He was wondered if it would be best to give Mr. Turner the news in person or over the phone. He didn't want to tell him in person. He couldn't take seeing Mr. Turner break down. He had just lost his wife and now his granddaughter.

"Are you all right, Sheriff? You've been quiet ever since we left the accident," Tom said.

"I know. I'm just thinking about Mr. Turner and Sarah. She was one of Taylor's friends, you know."

"Was she? I didn't know that," Tom said.

"Yeah. They grew up together. Her mother and my Mary used to go to church together. Now I have to tell Mr. Turner about his granddaughter. It's not going to be easy. This is the part of the job I hate." "I'm glad it's you not me, sir," Tom said.

They drove down Main Street, and the sheriff tossed the words around in his mind. Then he said, "Turn around, Deputy. I think I'll tell him in person." The deputy made a U-turn, and they began to drive to Mr. Turner's house. The sky was still gray from the rain clouds that hung overhead.

The sheriff's heart began to pound as they drove up to Mr. Turner's house. The street was empty and quiet. The storm had knocked down a couple of trees two doors down, but there were no other damages. The sheriff got out of his car, took a deep breath, and walked up to the door.

He looked at Tom who was standing beside him and then rang the doorbell and waited for Mr. Turner to answer. He waited a few minutes, but there was no answer, so he rang the bell again. Mr. Turner opened the door after what seemed like an eternity.

"Daniel," he said with a smile. "What brings you by? I was in the basement turning my lights back on ... Blew a fuse."

Sheriff Murphy arched his eyes browse and bit his lip as he looked at Mr. Turner. Mr. Turner stopped smiling as he read the expression on the sheriff's face.

"Is everything all right, Sheriff?" he said as he began to get worried.

"No. I'm afraid not, sir," the sheriff said politely.

"What is it? Come out with it, man," Mr. Turner shouted. "It's Sarah."

"What about Sarah?"

"Sarah was involved in a car accident … I'm afraid she didn't make it." "What? My Sarah … a car accident? You mean she's …"

"I'm afraid so, sir."

Mr. Turner began to wobble. He sank to the floor as the sheriff and the deputy caught him and led him over to the couch.

"My Sarah, my Sarah," he cried.

"Is there something I can get for you, sir?" the sheriff asked. "Go get him some water, Tom."

Tom went to the kitchen to get some water. The sheriff's heart sank as he looked at the state Mr. Turner was in. Sarah was the same age as Taylor, and Taylor was running around with that fool Anton.

Taylor could be next, the sheriff thought to himself. *These kids don't value life. They think they are going to live forever.* He gently patted Mr. Turner on the shoulder as thoughts raced through his head. *Anton is reckless just like that Eddie Fisher. It's only a matter of time before he gets behind the wheel drunk, and Taylor might be with him.*

"Is there anyone I can call, Mr. Turner?" the sheriff asked.

"I have to call her mother. She lives in New York now, but she won't be home till late."

"I'll call her for you if you want me to," the sheriff said. "No, I better call her. It would be better coming from me." "Are you all right?"

"I'm fine now, Sheriff."

"We'll come back by to check on you tomorrow. If you need anything, don't hesitate to call. Call me at home. I'll come right over." "Thank you, Sheriff."

Chapter 25

SHERIFF MURPHY DROVE down Ninth Street thinking about Sarah. He wanted to tell Taylor what had happened to Sarah and tell her about Eddie Fisher. He wanted to plead with her to stop this obsession with Anton. How could he make her see that Anton was a reckless fool, and one day it might be her who loses her life? "Help me, Mary. Give me a sign our baby is in trouble," he said as he turned onto Pine. He drove up to the house and noticed that Taylor's car was parked out front. He pulled up in the driveway and got out. He looked down the street and saw two downed trees from the storm, but the area looked quiet.

He looked in his yard and saw paper, branches, and other debris on the lawn. He went over and picked up the paper and branches and straightened up the yard. He walked around to the back and put the garbage in the garbage can and looked at the patio furniture, which was tossed around from the storm. He straightened the furniture and walked back around to the front. He took out his cell phone and called the sheriff's office. Gloria answer on the second ring.

"Gloria, this is Sheriff Murphy. Tell Sam and Jerry that I am at home. I'm done for today. Tell them I'll see them tomorrow." "Will do, Sheriff," Gloria said.

*****

Mrs. Smith was putting a load of laundry in the washing machine when the phone rang. She hurried over and answered it.

"Hello?" she said

"Joan, this is Linda."

"Linda, I was just thinking about you," Mrs. Smith said

"Is Anton still over at the sheriff's house?"

"No, he left about an hour ago," Mrs. Smith said, walking up to the window.

"I know he should be gone. It's about time for the sheriff to come home," Mrs. Johnson said.

"Yes. He's home right now. I see him working in the yard," Mrs. Smith said. "I wonder how he would react if I told him Anton was over." "You wouldn't," Mrs. Johnson said.

"I would, and I will. Let me call you back, Linda. I have to catch him before he goes inside." Mrs. Smith hung up quickly. She started the washing machine, put on her coat and boots, grabbed her keys, and hurried to the front door. She stood on her porch and looked over at the sheriff, who was still picking up paper from his lawn. She walked down the stairs and slowly crossed the street.

The sheriff saw Mrs. Smith crossing the street but pretended not to see her. *Here comes Mrs. Smith—Mrs. Gossiping Busybody*, he thought as he picked up the paper. *What does she want now? Who is she going to talk about?* he wondered. He continued to pick up the debris from his lawn.

"Sheriff," Mrs. Smith called.

The sheriff stopped and looked up. "Yes, Mrs. Smith."

"How was your day, Sheriff?" Mrs. Smith said as she walked up to him. "It went rather well. Thank you, Mrs. Smith."

"Are they having the annual town hall meeting this year?" she asked. "I haven't seen anything posted around town."

"Yes, next month. Councilwoman Bernadette Harris is sponsoring it. If you have any questions or concerns, contact her office."

"Someone has been knocking down my garbage cans, Sheriff," Mrs. Smith said. "For two days now all my garbage has been spread all over the yard."

"I'll look into it. It's probably some raccoons," the sheriff said.

"Or kids," Mrs. Smith said. "Those Sanchez kids have been running all over the place lately, Sheriff. I saw that José boy—you know, the biggest one—drawing graffiti on the wall behind the library." "I'll look into it," the sheriff said.

"You know this town used to be a quiet town. Now those wild Sanchez kids and other hoodlums are really bringing the place down."

"It's not that bad. The Sanchez kids are still little, but if you think they are getting into your garbage, I'll look into it."

"Thank you, Sheriff." Mrs. Smith smiled and looked at the sheriff as he continued to pick up paper off the ground.

The sheriff stopped and looked at Mrs. Smith.

"How is Taylor, Sheriff?" Mrs. Smith asked with a smile. "She's doing great," the sheriff answered.

"I see she's seeing Anton. He came over today."

The sheriff's eyes widened, and then he pressed his lips together and tightened his fist.

"He came over? Anton came here today?" he repeated.

"Yes," Mrs. Smith said, trying to read his expression. "He stayed for about two hours. He just left at about five."

"I see," the sheriff said as he turned and looked at the house. "Did Taylor leave with him?"

"No. She's in the house as far as I can tell."

The sheriff's face began to turn red, and he pulled at his collar. Mrs. Smith knew that she had struck a chord.

"Well, I better be getting back to my wash," she said, smiling as she turned and walked away.

The sheriff watched her as she walked back over to her house and disappeared inside her front door.

Anton was in my house, he thought as he looked up at his front door. *Taylor knows I don't want her to have company over when I'm not home, especially not boys, and especially not that Anton. He was in my house doing God knows what. This is it—I have had it. No more Mr. Nice Guy. If this is what Taylor wants for her life, then so be it. She's not going to do whatever the hell she wants to do under my roof. She's getting out of here today. I'm not going to have it.* He paced back and forth in the yard, looking at the door and checking for his keys.

Mrs. Smith walked to her phone and called Mrs. Johnson. "Hello?" Mrs. Johnson answered

"Hello, Linda. This is Joan."

"Did you tell him?"

"I did," Mrs. Smith said. "He was surprised and then angry. I knew I struck a chord, so I came home. He was boiling." "Poor Taylor," Mrs. Johnson said.

"I know. It looks like he's going to kill her."

"Maybe you shouldn't have told," Mrs. Johnson said.

"I probably shouldn't have, but it's done now. The sheriff knows. I can't undo it."

"He's not going to hurt her, is he?" Mrs. Johnson asked.

"No. He won't hurt Taylor, but Anton on the other hand ... I feel bad now," Mrs. Smith said. "I hope things will be all right."

"Well, keep watch, and let me know if you hear anything."

"I will, Linda," Mrs. Smith said. She hung up the phone and went over to the window where she could look out across the street and saw the sheriff still standing in the yard.

Maybe I shouldn't have told him, she thought as she watched him pace back and forth. *Why don't you mind your own business some time? Taylor is a good girl. You've known her all her life. Anton being there was probably innocent. Whatever it was, it was none of your business. You probably broke up their family.* "You should really mind your own business," she said aloud as she looked out at the sheriff's house.

The sheriff's blood was boiling. He pulled his keys out of his pocket, opened the front door, and stepped inside the house.

Chapter 26

TAYLOR WAS WATCHING reports of storm damage on the evening news. Power lines were down, rooftops were damaged, and trees had fallen, blocking side streets. Taylor couldn't believe so much damage could occur in such a short amount of time. She went into the kitchen and began to warm up her father's dinner.

It was nine o'clock, and he hadn't returned home. She reached out to turn on the stove burner when she noticed her hands were shaking, and a nervous feeling rose from her stomach to her chest. Anton had left her house. He had showed up unexpectedly. Taylor talked to him for a little while and then told him he had to leave immediately—before her father showed up. Her knees began to shake at the thought of what might have happened if Anton had been there when her father came home. Taylor felt her way to the kitchen island and sat down. Her head was spinning now, and it felt as though she was going to throw up.

She liked Anton and believed he was a good person, but she knew how badly her father despised him. And as much as she hated disobeying her father, she felt it was time she made her own decisions.

Just then, Taylor heard the front door open and then slam shut. "Taylor!" her father shouted to the top of his voice.

Taylor's stomach turned in knots as she rose slowly from her seat. Her knees began to wobble, and her feet felt like they were weighed down in concrete.

"Taylor!"

Taylor slowly walked into the living room entrance and looked at her father, who was pacing back and forth in the middle of the living room. He looked at Taylor with disappointment and disgust in his eyes. He shook his head and raised his finger before shaking it at Taylor. "Did you let that boy in my house?"

Taylor's heart sank. Her head began to spin, and she was shocked. She didn't know how her father had found out.

"He only came to the door, Daddy. I told him he had to leave."

Sheriff Murphy's face turned red. He kicked at the couch and then turned and stormed at Taylor. Taylor moved back as her heart rose in her throat and her eyes widened. Then she shut them tight.

"Don't you ever, as long as you live, bring that hoodlum in my house again." He leaned down and put his face in Taylor's. "I told you about seeing that boy! Anton is a criminal, a felon. He doesn't stand for anything, and he will never stand for anything. That no-good bastard is going to drag you down with him! "You had a good reputation in this town as a nice young lady, but you are going to let Anton ruin all of that for you! You aren't going to be any better than those whores who hang out at Leo's!"

Taylor stepped back and looked at her father.

"Well I'm not going to stand by and watch you ruin your life! You can't stay here and continue to see that bastard!" Then he walked to the living room entrance and turned. "Not here! Get out!"

Taylor's heart rose to her throat, and tears formed in her eyes. For the first time since she had been at it with her father, she was at a loss for words. Her father looked at her, but he was too angry to see the hurt in her eyes. He straightened his clothes, walked out of the living room, and slammed the door to his bedroom.

Taylor began to cry as she walked to her room and closed the door. She sat on the bed, and a pain formed in her stomach as the room began to spin. She wanted to plead with her father, but she didn't want to lose Anton. She wasn't ready to move out. She had no place to go, but what her father said was clear. Either she had to give up seeing Anton or get out.

Taylor stood up, went to the closet, and gathered some of her clothes. Next, she went to the bathroom for her toiletries and packed them in a duffle bag. When she was done, she slowly walked to the front door. The rain was coming down like marbles, and the lightning stretched far across the sky like an electric river. Taylor ran to her car and climbed inside. She tried to call Anton, but his phone went to voice mail.

Chapter 27

THE RAIN WAS falling heavily on the rooftops, and the thunder rumbled across the sky. Taylor ducked into her car and pulled out her cell phone. She called Anton, but his phone went to voice mail. She started her car and drove down Main Street to Leo's. She circled the parking lot but didn't see Anton's car. The rain was coming down harder, and she did not want to get out in it. The bar doors were closed, but Taylor could see people moving around through the windows.

She pulled out her phone again and called Anton once more, but his phone went to voice mail. She then started the car and drove to the auto shop. When she got there, the garage was closed. The whole place looked like a ghost town. She wanted to drive to his apartment, but she wasn't sure of his exact address. *I know he lives on Logan and River Road*, she thought, but she didn't want to chance it. *Maybe he's at the diner.*

Taylor drove down Main Street. The lightning lit up the night sky, and Taylor sped up to get to the diner and out of the rain. She turned on the radio and search for some music to listen to. She wanted to keep her mind off her father, but his voice still rang in her head.

"You have to leave my house." His words danced around her head like mice fighting over cheese. Tears formed in her eyes, and a lump grew in her throat.

"Why can't Daddy understand? Why can't he see things my way?" she cried. She finally arrived at the diner and parked her car. Grabbing her umbrella, she darted from the car to the diner. Zoe was pouring Mr. Jackson some coffee when she looked up and saw Taylor come through the door. Her heart skipped a beat, and her eyes widened.

"Taylor!" she yelled. "What are you doing out tonight?!"

Mr. Jackson looked surprise to see anyone out on a night like this. Taylor walked up to Zoe and whispered. "Can we talk?"

Zoe nodded her head yes, walked over to the counter, and set down the coffee pot. She took Taylor to the booth in the back by the jukebox. Taylor sat down and began to cry. Zoe's heart sunk, because she knew it had something to do with Taylor's father.

"Anton came to my house this afternoon," she said. "He didn't stay long. I only talked to him for a little while. Then I told him that he better leave. He did—he left—but when my father came home, he knew somehow. He was angry and yelled and screamed at me like I'd done something with Anton. Then he told me I had to leave his house." Zoe's eyes widened. She couldn't believe what she'd just heard.

"Leave your house?" she whispered. "Your father actually put you out on a night like this?"

"Yes," Taylor said. "I can't find Anton, and I don't have anywhere to go." "I know your father can be short-tempered at times, but I never thought that he would be this cruel," Zoe said as she handed Taylor a napkin to wipe her nose. "Anton was just here about an hour ago. He was with Mike. Give him another call."

Taylor pulled out her phone and called Anton, but his phone still went to voice mail. "It keeps going to voice mail," she said, sobbing.

Just then, an older couple walked through the door whom Zoe didn't recognize. "I'll be right back," she said to Taylor.

"Hi," Zoe said, walking to the couple. "A seat for two?" She led the couple to a booth by the front door and handed them two menus.

"Would you like something to drink?"

"I'll have an iced tea," the older woman said. "I'll have a coffee—black," the man said.

"Coming right up." Zoe went to the counter where she poured a glass of iced tea and grabbed a coffee pot and then headed back to the couple.

"Are you ready to order?" she asked.

"Yes, we are," the man said. "She'll have the spaghetti dinner, and I'll have the meatloaf."

"Coming up," Zoe said as she wrote down the order. She walked behind the counter and gave the order to Max.

"Zoe," Mr. Jackson called. "Can I have another cup of coffee? And I think I'll try the apple pie."

"Do you want it à la mode?" "No, just the pie."

Zoe gave Mr. Jackson his coffee and pie and then went back to the window to pick up the older couple's order. She gave the couple their food. "Will that be all?" she asked.

"Yes," the man said. "For now."

Zoe then walked back over to Taylor, who was trying to call Anton again, but his phone kept going to voice mail. She cried.

"Let me call my mother," Zoe said. "maybe you could stay a couple of days at my house." She walked over to the jukebox and called her mother.

Taylor's head was spinning, and her stomach had knots. She prayed that Zoe's mother would say she could stay. She didn't know any reason why she would say no. Zoe and Taylor had been friends since the third grade.

Zoe walked back over to Taylor. "My mom said that you could stay. I didn't give her all the details, but she said that it's okay. You can stay here with me until I get off tonight, and then we can head over to my place together."

Taylor began to feel better. She wiped her eyes and blew her nose.

"I'll stay until I get in touch with Anton," she said. "I just don't know where he is right now."

"That's okay, Taylor. He'll show up. Why did Anton come by your house today anyway?" Zoe asked seriously.

Taylor smiled and wiped at her eyes. "He said he wanted to see me and tell me he was getting serious about us. He thinks he love me."

Zoe's eyes widened. Still, she couldn't help but think about what Jonathan had said early that day. "Well, do you believe him?" she asked.

Taylor looked at Zoe. She knew that Zoe didn't believe Anton and that she thought he was playing games. Her heart sunk. "He seemed serious. I don't think he would lie to me," she said angrily.

"I'm sorry, Taylor. I didn't mean to make you angry. Only you know if Anton is telling the truth." Zoe got up and went to the older couple and handed them their check. "Will that be all?" she asked, smiling.

"Yes." The couple got up and walked to the register.

Zoe rung up their bill and then walked back over to Taylor. "I have thirty minutes to go," she said. "I have to start cleaning up for Maria."

Zoe cleared the booth where the older couple had been sitting. She wiped off the counter and then swept the floor. Maria came in, and Zoe went to the back and collected her things. Taylor gathered her things and waited for Zoe. When Zoe reappeared, she said her goodbyes to Maria and Mr. Jackson.

"Do you want to follow behind me, Taylor?" she said as they walked out into the rain.

"I'll follow you," Taylor said as she got into her car. She waited until Zoe got in her car. As they pulled away from the diner, Taylor followed closely behind Zoe, who only lived a block away from Taylor. Taylor's heart sunk as she got close to her house. She thought about her father and wondered how he found out about Anton.

Who could have told him so quickly? she thought. *Who knew Anton was over at the house?* And then she thought about Mrs. Smith.

Chapter 28

THE SUN WAS shining brightly, flowers had bloomed, the grass was pretty and green, and the ground had dried from the previous day's rain. Anton was sitting on the back of the park bench with his feet on the seat watching a group of guys play basketball.

It was noon, and the heat had risen to the midnineties. Beads of sweat began to form on Anton's forehead. Mike and Frank walked up, and Anton stood and greeted them with a handshake and a hug. They then joined him on the back of the bench.

"Did you think about what we talked about?" Mike said as he raised his hand above his eyes to shield them from the sun.

"I thought about it, but I haven't made up my mind yet." "Come on … It will be easy money," Frank said.

"I have to give this a lot of thought," Anton said in a tone that meant he was serious.

He looked at Frank, and Frank eased back a little. He knew Anton was not playing around when he used that tone.

"We could all use some extra cash," Mike said, almost pleading with Anton. "I said I have to think about it."

"We can't do this without you, man." Mike pressed on. "We are a team." Just as he said that, the sheriff pulled up in his squad car, and he and Deputy Tom jumped out. They ran up to Anton and threw him on the ground. Sheriff Murphy put his knees on the back of Anton neck and began to put handcuffs on him.

"What did I do? What did I do?!" Anton cried as dirt and grass got into his mouth.

Deputy Tom looked at Frank and Mike. "Get out of here if you know what's good for you," he shouted as he put his hand on his gun.

Frank's heart rose to his throat, and his eyes widened with disbelief. Mike shook all over as they both jumped up and ran through the park and out of sight. Sheriff Murphy stood Anton up on his feet and then punched him in the stomach and threw him in the back of the squad car.

Anton's stomach rolled up in knots as the wall of pain traveled throughout his body. The sheriff and the deputy jumped in the car and took off speeding down the highway. Anton's eyes rolled, and he could still taste the dirt in his mouth as he tried to gather the strength to speak. Sheriff Murphy looked back at Anton, who was still dizzy from the punch he had received earlier.

"I have put up with you long enough. You have no regard for the law or any respect for yourself. You feel that you can do whatever the hell you want and don't have to answer to anyone, but you fucked up when you messed with me and mine. Do you think I'm going to let you mess around with my daughter and use her up like you used up those whores in town? I'm only going to tell you once to get the hell out of town and don't come back."

Anton looked out of the window and saw that Deputy Tom was driving him to the city limit.

"I'm going to make it easy for you. I'm going to give you a ride," the sheriff continued as the car sped down the highway.

Anton felt sick as the heat engulfed him in the back seat of the car. He pulled at the handcuffs and bit his bottom lip, making low squeaking sounds with his throat as the car sped farther and farther out of town. The car finally stopped, and Sheriff Murphy pulled Anton out the car. They were a hundred miles out into the desert. He took the handcuffs off Anton and pushed him down on the ground.

"Have a nice life," the sheriff said as he got back in the car and sped off.

Chapter 29

SHERIFF MURPHY AND Deputy Tom walked into the sheriff's office, and Murphy sat behind his desk.

"Did I get any calls, Gloria?" he asked as he took off his hat. "No, sir, not since you've been gone. It's been quiet all day," Gloria said. Deputy Tom flopped down in a chair in front of the sheriff's desk. "It's really hot outside," he laughed. "You think Anton is going to make it out of the desert okay?"

"I don't care. He could rot out there as far as I'm concerned," the sheriff said. "The nerve of that punk going into my house."

"He was just testing you," Tom said. "Well, I won't be tested."

Deputy Sam was looking for a file in a file cabinet next to the sheriff's office when he overheard Tom laughing about Anton.

"You see the look on Anton's face when we got back into the car to drive way?"

"I saw him. He tried to look like we were doing him wrong, but for too long Anton has been the center of all the trouble around here, and he has been messing with me. He has been trying me, but he's not going to invade my property and walk all over me and think I'm not going to say anything. If Taylor wants to throw her life away messing around with that punk, so be it, but she's not going to do it under my roof, so I hope the sun burns him alive out there in that desert," Murphy said as he leaned back and put his feet on the desk.

"Excuse me, Sheriff, but I couldn't help but hear that you dropped Anton off in the desert," Deputy Sam said as he stuck his head in the door.

The sheriff looked at Sam and grinned. "I sure did."

Sam's eyes widened, and then he looked at the sheriff. "How is he going to get back?"

The sheriff laughed. "Walk, crawl, or hop. I don't care." "Sheriff, you know it's a hundred degrees today?" "That's why today was the best day to do it."

"Sheriff, he could die out there." "So let him," Tom said, laughing.

"You know, Sheriff, that's wrong. You shouldn't have dropped Anton off in the desert like that. For what? Why did you do it?"

The sheriff stood up. "Because he's messing with me and mine. He's trying me. He's not interested in Taylor. He's just using her to get at me!" the sheriff yelled.

"Sheriff, don't you think that Anton just might be interested in Taylor? Taylor is a lovely girl. Don't you think that Anton might have some feelings for her?

"Have you heard Taylor complain about anything that Anton's done since they have been going out together?"

"No," the sheriff said. "But give Anton the chance, and he would do something to hurt her. But I'm not going to allow it."

"Sheriff, Taylor is twenty-two years old. Don't you think she can make good, sound decisions? You are selling yourself short if you don't think your parenting skills were good enough to teach her right from wrong."

"Taylor has good judgment. It's just that she's not using it right now. I have to help her—help her along. That's why I'm here—to keep her from making mistakes."

"And being with Anton is a big mistake," Tom said. "What did Anton do to you, Tom?" Sam asked.

"He hurt my cousin—put him in the hospital. When he threw that chair over that banister at the high school."

"You couldn't prove that it was Anton. Any one of those students at that school could have thrown that chair."

"I know it was Anton. He was the only one devious enough to do it. Now my cousin is on disability. He can't teach anymore."

"What I'm saying, Sheriff, is you are punishing Anton for his past. He has already paid for those crimes you claim he has done. You can't keep condemning a man for his past. Jesus forgave all sin. What if Jesus condemned you for your past and said you couldn't be forgiven? Then he wouldn't have died on the cross. But he died so that we could be forgiven and have a right to life with him in heaven. So like Jesus forgave us, we have to forgive one another," Sam said.

The sheriff looked at Sam, raised his hand over his head, and sat back down.

"I wasn't looking for a Bible lesson, Sam. It's just that Anton isn't good for Taylor. She's not experienced and doesn't know how to handle herself around a guy like him. I don't want to see her hurt."

"You have to give Anton a chance. And, Tom, you stop encouraging him. Anybody could have thrown that chair. Anton wasn't the only hothead at that school. I can name dozens of possibilities."

"Yeah, and they all hung out with Anton," Sheriff Murphy noted. "They are his buddies. This town used to be quiet until Anton and his mother got here."

"What does his mother have to do with it?" Sam asked. "She had that no-good son of a bitch," Tom snapped. "Tom, did you hear anything I just said?"

"I heard you, but that doesn't go for a person like Anton."

"The good news is for everybody. Sheriff, just think about what I said. Pray on it. Ask God to move that hate toward Anton out of your heart, and he will do it. When was the last time you went to Bible study or a prayer meeting?" Sam asked.

The sheriff laughed. "I'll think about what you said, but I don't need prayer and study."

"You pray too and ask God to move that malice in your heart, Tom," Sam said.

Tom looked at the sheriff and shook his head.

The sheriff leaned back in his chair and looked out the window. He was thinking about what Sam had said. It made sense. He didn't want to condemn a man for what he had already paid for, and if it was anybody else, he would probably have forgiven him. But it wasn't someone else. It was Anton, and he didn't want to let him off that easy.

"Sheriff, if you have any questions, please call me," Sam said. "I'm going home now. I have to take Helen to the mall." Sam walked to his desk, gathered his things, and walked out the door.

"I have to go to," the sheriff said. "I have to cook my own supper tonight since Taylor isn't at home."

"Where do you think she is, Sheriff?" Tom asked.

"She's over at Zoe's. Zoe's mother called me last night and told me Zoe was going to bring her home with her. I plan to let her stay there for a while, and then I'm going to go get her. She has to learn she can't just do whatever she wants. She has to learn to obey me. She was fine until she started seeing that jerk. Now all she does is yell at me. I'm trying to let her know that I'm not going to stand for it."

The sheriff stood up and grabbed his hat. "If anything comes up, I'll be at the house."

The sheriff thought about Sam and what he'd said about forgiveness. It played in his head like a broken record. He knew what Sam was saying was true, but he didn't want to let Anton off the hook just yet. He wanted to hold on to that hatred for little while longer, but Sam's words were melting the iceberg in his heart. He was beginning to feel angry, because he no longer had that malice in his heart toward Anton.

He stepped out the door into the evening heat and walked to his car.

Chapter 30

ANTON'S FACE TURNED dark red, and he could feel it tingle and burn. He looked at his arms, and a tingling and burning sensation traveled down his arms. He took a head wrap from his pocket and tied it around his head. The sun was high, and its ultraviolet light shone all over the Chihuahuan Desert. There was no shade in sight. Anton walked along the asphalt road, hoping to see a car pass through, but there wasn't a car in sight. He felt in his pocket for his cell phone, but it wasn't there.

He must have dropped it when the sheriff threw him down. He looked all around, but there was no sign of life. He began to worry. What was he going to do? How was he going to get home? He had no water, no sunscreen, and no phone. He pressed his lips together and squinted his eyes. He kicked at the rocks on the asphalt road as he walked. Anger rose up inside of him, and all he could think about was getting even with the sheriff.

"If I catch that Tom alone, I'm going to kill him," he said. "That damn sheriff … Who the hell does he think he is? I hate that son of a bitch. He thinks he's God, but I'm going to show him. I don't scare off that easily."

Something in Anton's stomach jumped, and his head began to spin. He looked down toward the ground, and it looked as though it were moving. Anton sat on the ground next to the road.

"I better sit here and wait for someone to come along," he said.

"Someone has to." He checked his watch and saw it was a 3:45.

"I've been out here two hours already," he said. He thought about Taylor and how the sheriff must have treated her. "What did he do to

Taylor if he did this to me? I will show him. We're going to Vegas and getting married."

Anton looked down the road and saw a white car in the distance. His heart leaped, and he smiled.

"Here comes someone!" He took his head wrap off and stood up. He felt a little wobbly as he swayed back and forth. He straightened up his clothes and waited for the car to get closer.

*****

Mr. Turner was on his way to San Juan to visit his sister, Virginia. Their family had lived in San Juan for more than three generations. He moved to Dallas right after medical school, which had been more than forty years earlier. Every other weekend he visited his sister and her family in their parents' old house in San Juan. He looked forward to visiting, as she cooked his favorite dish, beef Wellington, just like their mother used to make. Their mother had died about ten years ago, and that's when Virginia had moved into her house on the east end of town.

Mr. Turner loved to go back to where he grew up. Things in San Juan were exactly the way they had been fifty years ago, and it made Mr. Turner feel good.

*****

The white car was getting closer. As Anton stuck out his thumb and waited for the car to approach him, Mr. Turner looked.

"Is that a young man out here in the desert?" he said. "Should I stop and help him?" He looked at Anton saw he was desperate.

Mr. Turner looked around and didn't see anyone else. *He looks harmless*, he thought to himself. *I don't want to just leave him.*

Mr. Turner slowed down and stopped, and Anton walked up to the car. "Hi," he said.

"Could you give me a ride into town?" Anton asked. "Where are you headed?"

"I'm headed to San Juan," Anton told him. "I'm going that way too."

"If you give me a ride, I can pay you when we get to town."

"I guess I could give you a ride," Mr. Turner said. "Get in."

Anton climbed in the passenger's side of the car, and the man took off driving down the road to San Juan.

"Do you want some water? I have a fresh bottle in the back," he said.

"Yes. Thank you, sir," Anton said.

He reached in the back, opened a cooler, and grabbed a bottle of water. Anton opened it and took a swallow. The cool sensation going down his throat was like swimming in the ocean. Anton took another swallow.

"How did you get way out here in the desert?" Mr. Turner asked. "I didn't see a car."

"It's a long story," Anton said, "and it's pretty stupid."

"Well, tell me your story, I'm all ears," the man said. "We have an hour before we get to San Juan."

Anton took another swallow of his water and told the Mr. Turner the whole story.

Mr. Turner laughed.

"See. I told you it was stupid."

"No, it's not stupid," Mr. Turner said. "You're in love. That's nice. What I wouldn't give to be young again."

Anton and Mr. Turner arrived in San Juan at six o'clock. They drove down Main Street, and Mr. Turner dropped Anton off in front of the diner. "Well thank you for the ride, sir," Anton said. "Do you want anything? I can pay you."

"No," Mr. Turner said. "It was my pleasure. Don't give up on your girl. Keep fighting for what you want." "Nice meeting you," Anton said.

"Good luck," Mr. Turner said before continuing along Main Street. Anton looked in the diner but saw it was empty, so he crossed the street and went home. Anton entered his apartment and turned on the lights. His blood was still boiling from what had happened. He kicked off his shoes and walked over to the kitchen counter. His face still tingled and burned.

He could hear the sheriff's voice in his head: "Stay away from my house." Anton pulled off his dirty, sweaty shirt and threw it in the clothes hamper and then pulled off his jeans and went to the bathroom where he turned on the shower. He stepped under the running water and washed the sweat and dirt from the desert off of him. The shower was cool and refreshing, and it relaxed him. He got out and wrapped a towel around his waist before finding the phone and calling Mike.

"I'm almost there," Mike said.

Anton hung up the phone, went to his room, and put on some clean clothes.

Mike and Frank knocked on the door, and Anton walked over and open it.

"Man, that sheriff was hot," Frank said as he walked through the door. "I told you," Mike said. "I told you to leave that girl alone. If the sheriff doesn't like you, he'll make things hard for you."

"I'm not going to stop seeing Taylor because her father doesn't like me," Anton said. "I haven't done anything wrong. I love Taylor, and she loves me."

"Come on ... You love her? Just the other day you said you were only using her to get back at the sheriff," Mike said.

"I know what I said, but I changed my mind. I have feelings for Taylor now. She's not like those other girls. I can actually talk to her. I can't explain it, but I love her," he said.

"Anton, you have to focus. You're going to let things get in the way of our plans."

"I'm not stopping you two. If you want to do that thing with James, go right ahead. I'm not stopping you."

"But we need you. We are a team. You know we can't do this without you," Mike pleaded.

"I said I have to think about it, Mike," Anton said. "Right now, I have other problems."

"You won't have those problems if you leave Taylor alone. The sheriff will stop breathing down your neck, and you can focus on our plans."

"Taylor is my girl now. I just can't drop her. I don't want to. I'll figure things out. You just have to give me a chance, Mike," Anton said.

Mike looked at Frank, who just shook his head.

"Well, would you hurry up and give us an answer, so we can go ahead with our plans?" Mike said.

"I'll let you know."

Chapter 31

TAYLOR HELPED CLEAR the dinner dishes from the dining room table, She scraped them in the dishwasher.

"Thanks again, Zoe, for letting me stay over last night," Taylor said. "It was really bad. I don't know what I would have done without you." "That's what friends are for," Zoe said with a smile.

"Are you going to give your father a call?" Mrs. Rogers asked as she got up from the table and walked to the living room.

"I was going to call him later. I want to give him a chance to cool off. He was really angry over nothing."

"Well, your father is concerned for your well-being, Taylor," Mrs. Rogers said. "You have to remember he can see the big picture when you probably can't right now."

"I just want him to give Anton a chance," Taylor noted. "I didn't mean to disrespect him."

"What you need to do, Taylor, is go home and have a long talk with your father. And you need to slow down and really think about what you are doing and getting yourself into ... You need to pray. Do you want to talk to Reverend Andrews? He could pray with you."

Taylor looked at Zoe. She knew that prayer could help. It had helped her in the past when her mother died, and it had helped when she wanted to get a high score on her SAT, but she'd never really needed help for anything else.

What if God says no? What if God says Anton isn't right for me? The thought scared her.

"I'll give him a call later," Taylor said. "Right now I just need to get my head straight." Taylor headed for the kitchen and sat down at the kitchen island. Zoe followed right behind her.

"Why is everyone so against Anton?" she whispered. "Who are you talking about?" Zoe asked.

"Your mother."

"Mom doesn't mean any harm. She just wants the best for you. You know my mother and your mother went way back, and she doesn't want to see you hurt, especially when your mother isn't here to protect you."

"I know," Taylor admitted. "It just seems like everyone is against us." Zoe put the remainder of the food in storage bowls and placed them in the refrigerator. Taylor sat at the island and watched as Zoe straightened up the kitchen. She wanted to call her father, but she was afraid of what he might say.

His voice exploded in her head like a loud cannon, and she could not turn it off no matter what she did. Her heart pounded, and she had butterflies in her stomach all night. She didn't fall asleep until four o'clock in the morning. Then she had to get up and go to school and work. Taylor tried to concentrate at school, but all she could see was her father's red face looking down on her.

He made her feel ashamed and dirty. She shouldn't have let Anton in her house, but it didn't matter, because Mrs. Smith was going to say that he was there anyway. She felt embarrassed that her father would think she and Anton had done something dirty in his house.

Taylor couldn't understand why her father didn't trust her or even know that she wouldn't do anything like that. She thought she wanted to be like Tammy and Ashley, but having a reputation like that made her feel bad.

"I think I'm going to try Anton one more time tonight before I turn in," Taylor said to Zoe as she got up and walked to the bedroom. She pulled out her cell phone and dialed Anton's number.

Anton was lying on the couch half asleep, thinking about Sheriff Murphy and Deputy Tom. When he heard what sounded like his cell phone, he rose up and listened. It was ringing, but it sounded far away. He stood up and looked around but didn't see it. He went into the kitchen, but it was not on the kitchen counter. He went into his bedroom and looked in his dresser drawer, but there was no phone.

Then the ringing stopped.

"This must be in my head," he said. "I'm hearing things."

Anton went back to the couch, lay down, and closed his eyes. He soon began to drift off. The scenery of the desert popped into his head, and he could see Sheriff Murphy laughing as they drove away, leaving him behind in the desert.

Anton jumped up, and his heart fluttered as a feeling of dread came over him. He rubbed his face with his two hands and sat on the couch with his head in his hand. Then he heard his phone ringing again.

"I'm not crazy!" he yelled.

This time he stood up and followed the sound. It was coming from the bathroom. He went into the bathroom, and the ringing got louder. He looked in the clothes hamper, pulled out yesterday's jeans, and looked in the back pocket. There was his phone.

He hurried to answer. "Hello?"

"Anton, this is Taylor. I've been trying to reach you all day." "I've been caught up," Anton said.

"Where are you?" Taylor asked.

"I'm at home," Anton answered, feeling a little angry. "Can I see you?" Taylor asked.

"You sure it's okay? I don't want to upset your father," Anton snapped. Taylor became quiet and took a deep breath. "My father kicked me out.

I don't have anywhere to go."

Anton's heart sank, and butterflies formed in his stomach.

"I looked for you all night in the rain. I don't know your exact address," she continued.

"I'm sorry to hear that," Anton said. "Do you want to come here with me?" "Yes," Taylor said as she began to cry.

"Where are you?" Anton asked. "I'm coming to get you." "I'm at Zoe's. I stayed the night with her."

"Don't worry ... I'm on my way." "Do you know where she lives?" "Give me her address," he said.

Taylor gave Anton Zoe's address. Anton quickly grabbed his keys and stormed out of the door. Taylor told Zoe that Anton was on his way. Zoe was surprised, but she didn't say anything. Mrs. Rogers had gone to her room, and Taylor had grabbed her things and gone to wait on the porch.

"Tell your mother I said thanks for everything," Taylor said.

Anton drove up in front of Zoe's house. He got out of the car and walked up to the porch. Taylor gathered her things and hugged Zoe goodbye. Zoe turned and went back into the house.

"Are you okay?" Anton asked as he hugged Taylor.

"Now I am," Taylor said. "My father can be a son of a bitch sometimes," she said, shaking her head.

"Your father beat me up in the park today," Anton said. "Then he drove me a hundred miles out into the desert and kicked me out of the car."

"Oh no!" Taylor said. "I'm sorry."

"That's okay. I don't scare easily," Anton said as he held on to Taylor.

"You love me, right?" he asked as he kissed her on the neck.

Taylor sunk into his arms. "I do," she said.

"Then we won't let anything stand in our way. To hell with your father." Anton found Taylor's lips, and they kissed.

"You want to live with me?" he asked, looking Taylor in the eyes.

"Yes," Taylor said as a warm sensation went all over her.

"I think we are ready to make that step," Anton said. "I think so too," Taylor said.

"You have your things?" "Yes."

"Then let's go."

Taylor got into her car and waited for Anton to pull away. She pulled out behind him and followed him to his apartment building. She parked her car, gathered her things, and followed Anton to his apartment.

"This is my place," he said as they walked through the door. "It's not much, but it's mine."

Taylor followed him in and looked around. To her amazement, it was a nice, clean place. She looked at the black leather couch sitting in the middle of the floor, the sixty-inch television, the stereo system, and what looked like a fish tank.

"What's that?" she said, pointing at the tank.

Anton grinned, took her by the hand, and led her to the tank. He turned on the light, and Taylor jumped when she saw the lizard through the glass.

"This is Charlie," Anton said, laughing. "You want to feed him?" He pulled out a coffee can and grabbed a fat worm.

Taylor screamed and ran over to the kitchen. Anton laughed and fed Charlie. He turned off the light and went to hug Taylor. "You wash your hands," Taylor demanded.

Anton grinned, went into the bathroom, and washed his hands. He told Taylor that she could put her stuff in the bedroom.

Taylor went into the bedroom and put away her things. Then she called Zoe, who answered on the first ring.

"Zoe, thank you, and thanks to your mother for everything you did."
"You're welcome," Zoe said. "Are you going to call your father?"
"I'm going to stop by the house after school tomorrow," Taylor said.
"I'll talk to him then."
"Okay," Zoe said. "Be safe, and don't do anything I wouldn't do."
"I won't." Taylor hung up the phone and went out into the living room. Anton was in the kitchen making sandwiches. "Want a sandwich?" he asked.

"Yes," Taylor said as she pulled a stool up to the counter and sat down.

Chapter 32

SHERIFF MURPHY WALKED into the grocery store and grabbed a cart. He'd been forced to do his own shopping since putting Taylor out. He knew he wanted some spaghetti, but he wasn't sure he could make it quite like Taylor. He had eaten at the diner for three nights straight, and he'd just eaten lunch there earlier that day. He didn't think he could stomach another meal there. He decided to cook at home that night, but he didn't have all the ingredients he needed. Having a home-cooked meal was enough to beg Taylor to come back home, but he wasn't going to give in that easily. Taylor had to learn the hard way that Anton was no good. Telling her wasn't enough.

She had become the talk of the town. She was part of every conversation that came out Mrs. Smith's lips.

If she wants to make a fool out of herself, then let her, the sheriff thought. *She'll come crawling back after Anton is done using her up, but she better have earned her degree, because she's not going to come and lay up on me.*

He pushed his cart down the pasta aisle, grabbed a box of spaghetti, and placed it in his cart.

"I'll get used to not having her around," he said. "I got used to not having her mother. If things get too out of control at the house, I'll hire a maid."

Next, he put two jars of pasta sauce in his cart. *Now, what is that bread Taylor usually gets?* he thought as he made his way to the bakery.

Taylor and Anton were in the bakery looking at the pies. They wanted to buy one for dinner that night. Taylor had decided to cook her famous meatloaf for Anton. She had made a home-cooked meal every night she had been at Anton's place, and Anton swore he could feel his jeans getting a little tight around the waist.

He enjoyed Taylor's company at the apartment. It felt as though they were newlyweds. They didn't worry about what people were saying, and the sheriff wasn't bothering them. Everything had been peaceful the whole week. That day they had met after Taylor got out of school and gone to the grocery store to get the things she needed for dinner.

Anton liked the way Taylor was. She kept things neat and in order just like him. Taylor liked being with Anton as well. All that stuff that everyone said about him wasn't true. He had been the perfect gentleman since she had been over, and he didn't pressure her to do anything she didn't feel comfortable doing.

As for her father, Taylor's nerves had finally settled down after the argument they'd had the other day. She had taken Mrs. Rogers's advice and had been praying about her situation. All she wanted to do was have a talk with her father. She tried several times to call him, but he always let the phone go to voice mail. She even called the office, but every time she did, Gloria would tell her that he was out or busy. She was thinking about going over to the house, but she hadn't made it there yet.

The sheriff pushed his cart to the bakery department, and when he got there, he saw Taylor and Anton putting an apple pie in their cart. He shook his head and went over by the baked bread. Taylor looked up, and her heart sank as she saw her father walk past her as if he didn't know her. She looked at Anton, who just kept looking at the pies.

Taylor walked over to her father, who was still looking over the bread. "Hi, Daddy," she said as she touched him on the shoulder.

The sheriff just stood there like he didn't hear her.

Taylor shrugged her shoulders and spoke again. "Hi, Daddy," she said a little louder.

Anton watched as her father put a loaf of Italian white bread in his cart. He then looked up at Taylor and pushed his cart to the cupcakes.

"Daddy!" Taylor screamed as tears ran down her face.

Anton went over to Taylor and grabbed her by the arm. "Come on," he said. "Don't cause a scene. Don't let that bastard get to you."

The sheriff put a box of cupcakes in his cart and continued to the produce section.

Deputy Sam was there paying for a cake his wife had ordered for dinner that night. He saw the way the sheriff treated Taylor. He put his cake in his cart and went to the register.

Taylor cried as she saw her father walk away like he had never known her or seen her before. Anton hugged Taylor and told her to stop crying so she didn't cause a scene.

The couple went to the register to check out. The sheriff continued his shopping as if nothing had happened. He put a couple of cans of tomato sauce in his cart.

Taylor is walking around with that punk as if they were married. She doesn't even care about what people are saying. She doesn't care about me or my reputation as the sheriff, just as long as she gets to do what she wants to do, he grumbled silently.

The sheriff watched Taylor and Anton pay for their stuff at checkout. "Of all the boys in this town, she had to settle for that scum," he said as he rolled his eyes. He walked around and put a few more items in his cart. "I thought my daughter had better sense than that. Now she's at that punk's house doing God knows what, and she's trying to talk to me as if nothing has happened. And Anton ... if he says one word to me, I'll break his neck. He knows not to confront me."

Taylor and Anton wheeled their cart out of the door, while the sheriff pushed his cart to the checkout. He slowly placed his items on the counter.

"Will that be all, sir?" Nancy said as he took out his credit card. "That's all I can think of right now," he said as he handed her the card. He looked out the window into the parking lot and saw Anton putting the groceries in the car. His stomach did flip-flops, and anger rose up inside of him. He grabbed his groceries and headed for the door.

Taylor and Anton were still putting their groceries in the trunk. Taylor's head was spinning, and a lump formed in her throat. "How could he do that to me?" she asked Anton.

Anton looked at her. "Because he's a self-righteous son of a bitch—that's how. He thinks he's better than everyone. I don't care if he never talks to me," he said.

"But that's my father," Taylor said. "He's never treated me like that before." Anton looked at Taylor and felt pity, because she had a self-righteous asshole for a father. "Just give him a little time. He'll come around," he said, trying to make her feel better.

They got in the car, and Anton watched as the sheriff pushed his cart to his car. *Let me meet that son of a bitch alone*, he thought as he started his car. *The only reason that punk is still alive is because he's the sheriff.*

Taylor looked at her father, and tears formed in her eyes. *I didn't mean to make him so angry*, she thought. *I don't know how to fix this.* She closed her eyes as Anton pulled off. *I guess I give him a little time*, she thought. *Lord, let my father come around and see things the way they really are.*

Anton turned on the radio to lighten the mood as he drove down Main Street. He stopped in front of the main outlet store that had a brown cowboy hat in the window.

"Look, Taylor," he said. "How would I look in that?"

Taylor laughed as he continued to drive down the street.

Chapter 33

SHERIFF MURPHY AND Deputy Sam were on the way to the diner when they got the call.

"Ambulance needed the Fitzpatrick residence."

Sheriff Murphy put on his siren and rushed to the scene. When he got there, Fire Chief Logan and two EMTs were walking up to Mrs. Fitzpatrick's door.

She was standing at the door waiting for the EMTs. "It's my husband," she said. "I think he's having a heart attack.

The EMTs rushed in and found Mr. Fitzpatrick lying on the floor. His face was turning a dark purple, and his eyes were closed.

"Mr. Fitzpatrick," Fire Chief Logan called as the EMTs began to work on him. "Mr. Fitzpatrick."

There was no response. Mrs. Fitzpatrick began to cry as she kneeled beside him. "Bob!" she yelled.

Sheriff Murphy grabbed her by the arm and led her to the couch to sit down. "Let the EMTs do their job," he said, trying to console her. "Can you tell me what happened?" he asked.

"Bob and I were having lunch when he said he felt dizzy. He walked in here—into the living room—and collapsed on the floor. He was fine this morning," she said.

The EMTs used a defibrillator, and Mr. Fitzpatrick's heart began to respond. They put him in the ambulance, and Mrs. Fitzpatrick joined him. Deputy Sam and Sheriff Murphy followed behind the ambulance on the way to the hospital.

The emergency room was crowded, but they rushed Mr. Fitzpatrick to the back. Doctors and nurses ran in the room from every direction. Mrs. Fitzpatrick tried to go in the room, but one of the nurses told her to stay back in the waiting area. Sheriff Murphy grabbed Mrs. Fitzpatrick by the arm and led her to a row of chairs in the waiting room.

"Do you want some coffee?" he asked softly as he patted Mrs. Fitzpatrick on the back.

"Yes, please," she said, wiping at the tears on her cheeks.

Sheriff Murphy walked over to the row of vending machines, put in a dollar, and selected coffee. He bought himself a cup as well. He took Mrs. Fitzpatrick her coffee.

"Everything's going to be all right," he said as he handed her the coffee. Mrs. Fitzpatrick took a sip and then started to cry. "I don't understand. Everything was fine this morning. Bob is the healthy one. He has never been sick in his life. I'm the one who is always in the hospital. I always thought I would be the one to go first."

"Don't talk like that, Mrs. Fitzpatrick. No one is going anywhere," the sheriff said as he sat down next to her.

Deputy Sam passed back and forth by the emergency room entrance. A doctor entered the waiting room and called for Mrs. Fitzpatrick. She stood up and walked slowly to the doctor.

"Your husband has had a heart attack," he said. "He is in stable condition. You can go back and see him now."

Mrs. Fitzpatrick hugged the sheriff and went to the room where her husband was. The sheriff and Sam went back to the squad car.

Deputy Sam drove, while Sheriff Murphy sat in the passenger's seat.

"Sheriff, are you and Taylor all right?" Sam asked.

"We're fine," the sheriff snapped through clenched teeth.

Sam took a deep breath. "I couldn't help but notice what happened yesterday at the grocery store."

The sheriff looked at Sam. "We are fine," he said, growing angry.

Sam stopped the car and pulled over to the curve. "Daniel, if you need to talk, I'm right here." Murphy looked at him.

"Obviously something is wrong. You're not speaking to your daughter."

Sheriff Murphy dropped his head. "I kicked her out ... Well, I told her it would be best if she left my house." "Sheriff," Sam said.

"Everything was fine. She went over to Zoe's, and I was going to go get her the next day. But then she moved in with Anton after everything I told her. She still ended up with that punk, and now everything's going to hell." "Sheriff, don't you think you pushed her into Anton's arms?" Sam questioned. "You went about this the wrong way. Sheriff, instead of talking to her and listening, you threatened, yelled, and called her names. Now you are not speaking to her. You are further driving her away. You have to realize that Taylor is a grown-up, and she's capable of making her own decisions. Of course, she's going to make mistakes, but we all make mistakes. Putting her out of her house was wrong. What you need to do is sit down and talk to Taylor and Anton and find out what their intentions are."

"That's easy for you to say. Your daughter is at home, safe and sound with your wife," the sheriff pointed out.

"Sheriff, if it were my daughter, I would talk to her and trust that I instilled in her enough knowledge that she could make good, sound decisions. Taylor is a good person. You instilled that knowledge in her. Now trust her enough to use it."

The sheriff looked at Sam. He began to feel bad about how he'd treated Taylor. He wanted to call her and tell her to come back home, but his pride got in the way. He wasn't ready to accept Anton yet. He wanted to hold on to that hatred a little while longer.

Sam looked at Murphy, but he was unsure that he was getting to him. "Why don't you give Taylor a call tonight?" he said as he started the car.

Murphy laughed. "Why is this suddenly my fault?" he asked.

"It's nobody's fault. It's just that you are going about this the wrong way." "So what am I supposed to do? Sit back and let that scum ruin my daughter?"

"Anton isn't the person he used to be. You have to give people a chance. Anton works every day, and he hasn't been in trouble since he got out of jail." "That's the whole thing right there, Sam. He's been in jail. He is a criminal who doesn't have an education, so that means he's going nowhere.

I had better dreams for my daughter than Anton. I don't see why you like him so much."

After thinking for a moment, the sheriff added, "I take that back. I do know why. It's because it's not your daughter he's ruining. It's mine." Sam shook his head.

"Just talk to Taylor. Tell her to come home—please."

Sheriff Murphy looked out the window and thought about the time he took Taylor fishing and how brave she was when she took the worm and wrapped it around the hook. He could hear her sweet voice calling him to tell him she had caught a fish. He dreamed of one day walking her down the aisle and growing old and playing with his grandchildren—something Mary would never be able to do.

He wanted to attend her college graduation and watch her receive her diploma. How proud he was going to be, but now it seemed like everything was going to hell. And it was all because of Anton. He had been a problem ever since he'd moved to town.

I have to find some way to stop him, the sheriff thought. *One way or another. I'm not going to let things go down like this. He may have Sam and Jerry fooled, but I know him. It's going to be just a matter of time before something happens, and then I'm going to run him out of town for good.*

Deputy Sam drove quietly back to the sheriff's office. He didn't know what else to say. He knew Murphy could be stubborn at times, but this was getting out of hand. They pulled into the parking lot, and the sheriff got out the car and walked into the station.

"How is Mr. Fitzpatrick?" Gloria asked as he went into his office.

"It looks like he's going to make it," the sheriff said as he closed the door. He took out his cell phone and brought up Taylor's number on the screen. He wanted to dial it, but instead, he put the phone back and got up from his desk.

"I'll be back in an hour," he told Gloria as he stormed out the door. He got in his squad car and drove to the west side of town. He pulled up to Anton's apartment building and parked the car. He looked up at Anton's window to see what he could see, but there was no movement in the window. The street was quiet. He wanted to go up there and get Taylor, but he had to restrain himself with every fiber of his being.

He thought about what Sam had said about forgiveness, and he thought about what Jerry had said about Anton changing his life. He wanted to believe it. He didn't want to fight with his daughter anymore. He wanted to accept the fact that Taylor was going with Anton and that everything was going to be all right.

He looked up at the window, but there still was no movement. He wanted to believe that things were going to be okay, but he couldn't. He couldn't forgive Anton. He couldn't forgive Taylor for letting Anton in his house and for dating him and not listening. He couldn't let go of the hatred in his heart for Anton. His head said he should go get his daughter, but his heart wanted to hold onto that bitter hatred that was tearing his family apart. Tears rolled down his face as he let the coldness in his heart win one more time. He started the car and drove back to the police station.

He hated himself more than he hated Anton.

Chapter 34

TAYLOR WAS SITTING in the school library trying to concentrate on her reading assignment, but her mind kept drifting back to the grocery store and how her father had treated her like a stranger. She wanted to call him, but she was scared that he would say something hurtful and hang up. Her head was spinning, her stomach was doing flip-flops, and she was having a hard time swallowing. She was tired too. She hadn't really slept for two days. Taylor had to work overtime to make enough money for day-to-day expenses and tuition. She had to do all of this—it couldn't wait. She only had a few short months left, and then she would be out of school. Taylor had to prove to herself that she could have it all. She wasn't going to let her father win.

Taylor squinted her eyes so she could see her book better, but every time she tried to read, she'd see her father's face.

I'll never get any work done at this rate, she thought to herself. *Is this what you want, Daddy? You want me to fail, so you could say, 'I told you so'? You want me to crawl back home and play with dolls, wear my hair in a ponytail, and be your baby for the rest of my life? Well I won't do it ... I want to be my own person.* Taylor began to cry, tears filling her eyes.

"I said I wasn't going to cry," she said aloud, becoming angry at herself. Taylor wiped at her tears and tried to focus on her book one more time. The library was quiet and unusually empty for a Friday afternoon. "That's what's wrong," Taylor said, looking around. "I need some distraction." She took her phone and put in her earbuds and began to play Ice Cube.

Taylor looked up at the library entrance and spotted Jonathan and Alex coming through the doors. She lowered her head, trying to hide, so they wouldn't see her. Jonathan saw her anyway and began walking in her direction.

"Hi, Taylor," he said, smiling as he flopped in the seat in front of her. Alex sat down next to him and took out his laptop. Taylor took out her earbuds and forced a smile.

"How are things going?" Jonathan asked.

"Things are fine," Taylor said, trying not to reveal that she'd been kicked out and was now staying with Anton.

"What are you doing?" Jonathan asked, looking at Taylor's book.

"I'm trying to study for an exam. I have in one of my nursing classes, but it's too quiet. I can't get any studying done."

"Are we distracting you?"

Taylor wanted to say yes, but she blurted out, "No. I could use the company." Jonathan smiled and pulled out a textbook. "We have an exam in US history on Monday," he said.

"Oh." Taylor looked down at her book as if she was reading when a shadow covered her page.

"Did you call your father?" Zoe asked, standing over Taylor.

Taylor looked up and squinted her eyes, trying to get Zoe to shut up, but Zoe kept talking.

"Did you call your father?" she asked again. "No," Taylor said. "Not yet."

"What?! It's been two weeks."

Jonathan looked from Zoe to Taylor. "What's been two weeks?" he asked. Zoe looked at Taylor. "You didn't tell him?" "Tell me what?" Jonathan asked.

"No ... I was getting around to it when you walked up." "Tell me what?" Jonathan asked again, looking at Taylor.

Taylor's face turned red, and her tongue felt thick. "My father kicked me out."

Jonathan's eyes grew wide, and he sat up straight in his seat. "What? Kicked you out?" Alex asked.

Taylor looked down. "Yes."

"When did this happen?" Jonathan asked.

"Two weeks ago."

"Two weeks?" Jonathan said. "Where have you been staying?" Taylor looked at Jonathan and then at Alex. "With Anton."

Jonathan's heart sank, and his head began to spin. He didn't know whether to be angry or feel sorry for Taylor. "You are staying with Anton?" he asked loudly as he slammed down his book.

"Yes," Taylor answered. "May I ask why?"

"Because I have no place else to go."

"That's not true," Jonathan said. "You have Zoe. You could even stay with me."

Taylor looked down. "Your mother wouldn't let me stay with you." "That's beside the point, Taylor. She would have made other arrangements until we figured something out."

"After everything I told you Anton said about you and your father, you still went over there to stay with that punk?"

Tears formed in Taylor's eyes. "He said he didn't mean those things, and that girl in the video is just a friend."

Jonathan looked at Alex and then clenched his teeth as anger boiled inside of him. "And you believe him?!" Taylor didn't say anything.

Jonathan wanted to get up and leave. He couldn't believe how stupid Taylor was being, but his heart went out for her. He didn't know why he still liked her.

"I tried talking to my father the other day, but he's not speaking to me," Taylor said. She told them about the incident at the grocery store and how her father let his phone go to voice mail whenever she called.

"Come on. Let's go," Jonathan said. "Where are we going?"

"I'm going to take you home."

"No. My father doesn't want me there," Taylor said. "I don't want to get you involved."

"Your father likes me," Jonathan said. "I can get through to him."

Taylor knew Jonathan was right, but she was thinking about what Anton might say. "I better wait until he cools down," she said.

"Taylor, you can come back over to my house until your father calms down," Zoe said.

"Thank you, Zoe. I think I'll do that."

"Well, let's go get your stuff and take it over to Zoe's," Jonathan said. "No. If you go over to Anton's house to get my stuff, it will end in a big fight," Taylor said. "I'll get my stuff tonight. I have to talk to Anton."

"What are you going to tell him?" Jonathan asked.

"I'm going to tell him I think it's a bad idea that we are staying together, and then I'm going to leave."

Jonathan began to calm down when he heard Taylor say those words. "I still think we should go over there with you," he noted.

"No, Jonathan. Let me do it my way," Taylor insisted. "That way, no one gets hurt." Taylor felt better about going back over to Zoe's, but she didn't want to hurt Anton either. She had to think of a way to let him down easy. "I better get going," she said as she gathered her books. "Goodbye."

Taylor hurried out the door.

Jonathan watched her go and then turned to Zoe. "Man, I can't believe this. Why didn't you call me when this first happened, Zoe?"

"I thought Taylor was going to tell you. She is so head over heels for Anton. She's not thinking of anyone else."

Jonathan's heart sunk when he heard Zoe say those words. "I thought I got through to her the other day when I told her about the redheaded girl," he said.

"Don't worry about it, buddy. Taylor will see the mistake she is making. You did the best you can," Alex said.

*****

When Taylor got back to Anton's house, he wasn't home yet. She put away her books, went into the bathroom, and turned on the shower. She stepped into the shower and let the hot water run all over her. When she was done, she got dressed and began fixing dinner.

Taylor rehearsed what she was going to say to Anton over and over in her head. She wanted to go back to Zoe's so she could make up with her father, but she didn't want to hurt Anton. How was she going to do that?

Butterflies formed in her stomach, and she began to feel week. She didn't want to leave, but there was no other way.

Maybe Anton would understand. Maybe he wouldn't make this difficult. For a long time, Taylor had wanted to be with Anton, but she didn't know that it was going to hurt a lot of people. She began to wonder if it was worth it. Was having something she wanted so badly worth hurting the people she loved? She set the table up nicely and was amazed that Anton had everything she needed. She moved around his apartment, finding everything like she had been there for years.

She liked Anton's apartment. It was just right for the two of them. Maybe under better circumstances they could live there together, but right now wasn't one of them. She finished dinner and ran and got dressed. She put some soft music on the stereo and waited for Anton to come home. Taylor sat on the couch and tried not to think about the past two weeks.

She closed her eyes and let the soft music take her away.

Chapter 35

ANTON COULDN'T STOP thinking about Sheriff Murphy and how badly he'd treated Taylor the other day. His heart went out to her. He couldn't imagine what it must have been like growing up with a father like that.

He couldn't understand why Taylor still defended the sheriff after what he'd done. It made Anton angry that the sheriff disliked him so much that he stopped talking to his only daughter and kicked her out. He finished up the car he was working on and began to close up the shop.

At that moment, Jerry walked through the door. "Anton, I'm glad I caught you," he said. "Can we talk?"

Anton looked at Jerry. "I was just about to close up. Give me a second." Anton closed the garage door and checked the register.

Jerry went in the back to the break room and sat down. He wanted to talk to Anton about the sheriff, but he didn't want to upset him. Sam had told him about the incident at the grocery store, and Alex had told him that Taylor was staying with Anton.

Deputy Sam was talking to Sheriff Murphy, trying to get through to him, so it was up to Deputy Jerry to get through to Anton. Anton finished closing up and went into the break room to talk to Jerry when a knot formed in his stomach. He knew that he wanted to talk to him about Taylor.

"How are the tires?" he said as he sat down, looking at Jerry forcing a smile.

"The tires are great, Anton. They couldn't be better."

"I'm glad," Anton said. "What can I do for you, Jerry?"

Jerry twirled his thumbs and looked at Anton nervously. "Anton, I heard that Taylor has been staying with you."

Anton's eyes widened, and then he got angry. "Yes. That no-good son of a bitch sheriff kicked her out."

"And you let her stay with you," Jerry said.

"Yes. I couldn't let her be out there on the street with nowhere to go. She's my girlfriend. I had to take her in."

"Anton, I know you want to do the right thing, but don't you think that letting Taylor stay with you is a little too much?" Jerry asked.

"What do you mean, Jerry? We are two grown people."

"I know that, Anton, but you're not married," Jerry pointed out. "People will talk."

"I don't care what people say. Taylor is my girlfriend, and I love her." "Well, if you loved her, you would send her home to her father, and you wouldn't want to put her through the embarrassment of people's rumors and lies. Anton, I know you love Taylor, but you have to do things the right way."

"But the sheriff doesn't want Taylor at his house," Anton said. "How do you know? Did he say that?"

"No, not to me. It was the way he acted the other day at the grocery store." "I'm sure if Taylor went home, her father would let her in," Jerry said. Anton listened to Jerry. He wanted to let Taylor stay with him, but he also wanted her to make up with her father And he didn't want her to be the subject of the rumors that floated around the town like water.

"Did you think about what I told you last time we met, Anton?" Jerry asked. Anton just looked at him for a minute. "Yes, I thought about it, and I read the verses too. It's just that it's hard to believe that that goes for everybody."

"Anton, God loves you, and if you ask him, he will forgive you. That goes for everybody in the whole world, not just for a few."

Anton listened to Jerry, and his heart leaped, and a sense of joy came over him. He thought about his father's letter, and he understood what it meant to forgive yourself.

Jerry looked at Anton and could see that a change came over him. He knew something had clicked inside of Anton.

"Salvation is for everyone. You just have to accept it," Jerry said.

Anton nodded his head yes as tears formed in his eyes.

"Do you want to pray with me?"

Anton jumped, and he looked at Jerry. "I haven't prayed in a long time," he said in a low voice.

"That's okay. Just bow your head." Jerry reached out his hand so Anton could hold it.

Anton gave Jerry his hand, and Jerry said a little prayer. Anton listened and asked the Lord to come into his life.

"Do you want to go to young adult service on Sunday?" Jerry asked. Anton thought about it for a minute. "Sure," he said.

Jerry's eyes widened. "That's great, Anton. Bring Taylor with you." "I will," Anton said.

"You could be Alex's guest," Jerry said. "The pastor will be glad to have you."

"If you say so," Anton said with a smile. "I have to go home and tell Taylor that I think she should go home, but I don't know how I'm going to do that. I don't want to hurt her."

"Do you want me to come with you?" Jerry asked.

"No. I better do this on my own. It was my idea that she come to my house. Now I have to let her down easy."

"I can go over with you and take her to the sheriff if you want me to," Jerry said.

"No. I better do it. I want her to understand that I'm doing it for the both of us."

"Well, if you need me, you know where to find me, Anton. And if Taylor wants to talk, I'd be happy to talk to her too." "Okay."

Jerry got up and gathered his things, and they both walked to the door. "I'll see you Sunday," Jerry said.

"I'll be there, Jerry," Anton replied. "Well, Taylor and I will be there." Jerry walked to his car and got inside. "That wasn't hard," he said as he drove away.

Anton locked the door of the garage and walked to his car. He thought about what Jerry had said about forgiveness, and he thought about the sheriff. He needed forgiveness too, so he could learn to forgive. Anton got in his car and drove down Main Street, trying to put together the right words to say to Taylor. He stopped in front of the flower shop and looked in the window.

"I'll give her a half dozen roses," he said to himself. "She'll like that. I've never bought her flowers before."

He went inside, and Ms. Sanchez was waiting on an older man. Anton looked around while he waited. He checked out the price of roses and compared them to lilies and daisies. *Roses are expensive. Taylor is beginning to cost me a fortune*, he thought.

The old man was finished with his purchase, and Anton looked at the beautiful bouquet of flowers he had purchased.

"May I help you, young man?" Ms. Sanchez asked. "Yes. First, how much is that bouquet of flowers?"

"That's thirty dollars, but you have to order it a day in advance." "Oh. Well, in that case, I'll take a half dozen of your red roses." "Would you like a card to go with your roses?" "Yes," Anton said.

"May I ask who these are for?"

Anton smiled. "They're for my girlfriend," he said. "Oh, she must be special," Ms. Sanchez said.

"Yes. She is pretty special. I want to surprise her."

"That's good." Ms. Sanchez wrapped up the roses for him. "What would you like to put on the card?"

Anton thought for a moment and then said, "To Taylor: These red roses are a token of my love for you."

He signed the card and gave Ms. Sanchez his debit card. After he was finished with the purchase, he walked back to his car. Then a lump came back in his throat. He knew he had to tell Taylor that he was taking her home, but he was afraid he would hurt her.

Chapter 36

THE SOFT MUSIC Taylor was playing on the stereo did little to ease her mind. She tossed what she was going to say to Anton over and over in her head. She sat on the couch, and Jonathan's voice rang in her head like a broken record.

"You have to go home, Taylor. You can't stay with Anton." She got up from the couch and began to pace the floor.

"I don't want to hurt Anton. I love him," she said. "Why can't people just leave us alone?"

She looked at her cell phone sitting on the table and wanted to call her father, but she was afraid that he would yell. Or worse yet, she was afraid he wouldn't pick up. She walked over to the kitchen and checked the temperature of the food one last time.

It was still pretty warm, so she went into the bathroom and checked her makeup. Her mascara wasn't running, and she looked okay, so she went back into the living room and sat on the couch. Her cell phone rang, and she hurried to pick it up. It was Zoe.

"Hello," she answered.

"Hey, Taylor. I was just calling to see how things were going," Zoe said. "I'm fine, but Anton hasn't made it home yet. I'm going to tell him to take me home after dinner. I cooked him a nice dinner, so he won't be upset. I was going to call my father, but I chickened out. I'm going to call him after I talk to Anton."

"Just tell Anton that you think you should go home and talk to your father. He should understand that, and if your father is still mad, you can come over to my place," Zoe said.

"I will," Taylor said with a smile.

Anton slowly opened the door and stuck his head inside. When he saw Taylor, he came all the way in. Taylor looked up and saw the roses, and her heart dropped.

"I have to go," she said to Zoe. "Anton just walked in." She pressed end on her phone and set it on the ottoman.

"Hey, baby," she said as she went over to Anton. He handed her the roses.

"These are beautiful," she said. "What are they for?" "Read the card," he instructed.

Taylor opened the card and read it. *How can I tell him I want to go home now?* she thought.

"This is so nice," she said. "Thank you. I cooked you a special dinner. Maybe we can eat it by candlelight."

Anton walked over to the table and saw how nice it was set up Then he smelled the food. His heart sank, and a lump rose in his throat. *I can't tell her to go home now*, he thought. *Everything looks so nice.* He inhaled, and the aroma of freshly baked garlic bread and pasta sauce hit his nose.

"Did you make spaghetti?" he said, a smile making its way across his face. "That's my favorite."

"I know," Taylor said, smiling back at him. Anton hugged her, and they kissed.

"Go wash your hands so we can eat," Taylor said.

"Okay," Anton said he headed for the bathroom and turned on the faucet. *I'll tell her tomorrow. No need to spoil things now*, he thought.

Taylor began to put the food on the table. *I'll tell him tomorrow. No need to spoil things now*, she thought.

Taylor put the roses in a vase and set them on the table.

Anton came out of the bathroom and went into the dining area, and they both sat down. Taylor lit the candles, and the light brightened the dark room. The aroma from the spaghetti filled the air, and Anton saw the roses sitting in the middle of the table. He couldn't bring himself to ask Taylor to leave. His head told him that it was the right thing to do, but his heart wouldn't let him.

No matter what he'd planned in the past, he loved Taylor now, and he realized she was the girl for him. He didn't want to be in bad with her father. He had to think of a way to get her father to come around, but he didn't know how he was going to do that. For now, all he could think of was telling Taylor to go back home until he could make her father see that he was sincere and really loved Taylor.

Taylor looked at Anton, and she realized that he loved her. She could see it in his eyes. This was a dream come true. All her adult life she'd wanted to be Anton's girl. Now she was, and only one thing stood in her way—her father. She had to make him see how Anton really was and that he was wrong. Anton was a good person.

Anton tasted the spaghetti, and it tasted like soft, creamy tomatoes. The garlic bread was buttery and cheesy, just like what his mother used to make. Not only was Taylor pretty and smart, but she was a good cook too. She would make a good wife one of these days.

*****

Sheriff Murphy was making himself a bologna sandwich. He split the kaiser roll, picked up five slices of bologna, and placed them on the roll. He added lettuce and tomatoes and spread mustard on it.

"Another night of bologna," he said as he walked over to the kitchen island to eat. "Why do you have to be so stubborn? Taylor could be here right now fixing you a nice dinner, and you would know that she's safe and sound. But no, you had other ideas."

He took a bite of his sandwich and continued mumbling to himself. "Sam was right. Maybe Anton has changed. Maybe I'm the asshole ... I'm worried about what everyone else is saying, and I'm not listening to Taylor. "That was really bad what you did at the grocery store. It was mean and evil. You are so stupid." He put down his sandwich.

"Taylor deserves better than that. You treated her like she was some kind of slut or something ... Stop this, stop this," he said, shaking his head. "That was for Taylor's own good. How else was she going to learn that Anton isn't right for her?" Murphy walked into the living room and looked out the window. "It wasn't right for you to do that." His heart sank, and tears formed in his eyes. He couldn't swallow the lump in his throat.

"I'm sorry, Taylor. I've been such a fool. I'm coming to get you tomorrow. I'm so sorry."

He walked over to the couch, sat down, and put his head in his hands. "Please forgive me, baby. Your father is a fool."

*****

Taylor and Anton finished cleaning up the kitchen and putting the food away. Taylor walked over to the case of DVDs near the television.

"Want to watch a movie?" she asked, strolling her fingers through the DVD titles.

"That sounds good," Anton said.

He walked over to the coat closet, reached up on the shelf, and took down his father's letter. He went over to the couch and took the letter out of the envelope.

Taylor started a movie in the DVD player and went over to sit next to Anton.

"What's that?" she asked.

"It's a letter from my father. I didn't understand it at first, but since I've been talking to Deputy Jerry, I understand it perfectly." "Can I read it?" Taylor asked.

"Sure," Anton said, handing her the letter.

Taylor read the letter and then looked at Anton. "That's deep," she said. "I'm not sure, but I think I'm becoming a believer."

Taylor's eyes widened, and her heart leaped. "That's great, Anton."

"I think I'm going to go to young adult service and talk to Pastor Andrews." "That's great," Taylor repeated.

"I want you to go with me. Maybe if we pray about it, your father will come around."

"I thought so too, Anton. Maybe we could have a meeting—you, me, my father, and Pastor Andrews."

"I'll call him tomorrow to schedule a meeting with him," Anton said. "He would help us, Anton," Taylor said. "Pastor Andrews is really cool. You are going to like him."

"I hope so," Anton said as they sat on the couch and watched the movie.

Chapter 37

LEO'S BAR WAS crowded, and every table was taken. Mike and Frank pushed their way to the back where Tammy and Ashley were sitting. Tammy and Ashley were already full of beers and were getting loose. Tammy was glad to see Mike. She wanted to be his girl, but he was only interested in having a good time.

Ashley didn't care for Frank as much. She had her sights on Anton, but he was seeing Taylor for the moment.

"Hey, baby," Tammy said as she hugged Mike.

Frank put his arm around Ashley's shoulder, and she slowly removed it. "What are you girls having? Mike asked.

"Beers," Tammy said.

"That sounds great. Let's get wasted!" Frank yelled.

He yelled for the bartender to bring them four beers. The music was loud. Tammy's heart was racing, and her head was spinning.

"Let's dance," she said as she pulled Mike to his feet.

Mike grabbed her by the waist, and they went over to the dance floor and began to dance. The room was spinning, and Tammy's stomach felt like she was on a roller coaster. She staggered back, and Mike grabbed her in his arms.

Frank was getting wasted off beer. He watched Tammy and Mike as they danced. He put his arm around Ashley, who was also wasted. She pushed him off and walked over to the other side of the table. The dance floor was getting crowded, and Tammy and Mike were dancing, hugging, and swaying to the music. Frank walked over to Ashley, put his arm around her neck, and kissed her. Ashley pushed him off again, and Frank's blood began to boil.

"What's wrong with you tonight, Ashley?" Frank asked. "I don't feel like it tonight, Frank," she said.

"You felt like it when you wanted my hundred dollars."

"I said I was going to pay you back. You don't have to keep throwing that in my face."

Frank was getting dizzy—the room was spinning, and his heart was pounding.

"I'm sorry, baby. Let's dance," he said as he grabbed Ashley by the waist. Knots formed in Ashley's stomach, and waves moved through her.

"Get off me!" she screamed as she tried to wiggle free.

Frank's face turned red, and he pressed his lips together. His chest felt tight as anger moved through him. "What's wrong with you tonight?!" he yelled.

"I don't want to dance with you!"

"What? Are you angry because Anton isn't here?" "Leave me alone, Frank!"

"Anton is with Taylor," Frank snapped back. "He doesn't want you!" Tears formed in Ashley eyes, and a lump grew in her throat.

"I'm sorry, baby," Frank said as he tried to kiss her.

"Leave me alone," she yelled and tried to push him away. "I don't want to dance with you. I don't want to kiss you. I don't even want to be seen with you. You are nothing but a coward. You will never be like Anton or Mike. You're pathetic, and I hate you!" Ashley screamed.

Frank went numb when he heard those words. The room started spinning, and it felt like everyone was looking and laughing at him. His blood was red-hot. He raised up his fist and hit Ashley. She fell backward, hitting her head on the table before collapsing to the floor.

Everyone stopped and ran up to Ashley as she lay stiff on the floor. Tears rolled down Frank's face as he realized what he had done. Mike and Tammy ran over to Ashley. Mike patted her on the cheeks, trying to wake her up.

The bartender came from behind the bar and kneeled on the floor to check Ashley's pulse. He then took his cell phone and dialed 911.

"I didn't mean it, Mike!" Frank cried.

"What's wrong with you? Are you stupid or something?!" Tammy yelled. "I didn't mean it … I didn't mean it … It happened so fast."

"Calm down, Frank," Mike said. "She'll be all right."

"Everybody get back and give her some room," the bartender said as he pushed back the crowd.

Fire Chief Logan and two EMTS arrived first. They ran over to Ashley and began to work on her. Sheriff Murphy and Deputy Tom came in soon after.

Sheriff Murphy looked down at Ashley and then up at Frank and Mike. "Could you tell me what went on here?" he asked the bartender.

"I don't know. That guy right there," he said, pointing to Frank, "and that girl lying on the floor got into a yelling match. He hit her, and she hit her head." The bartender just shook his head.

"I saw everything," a woman said as she walked up to the sheriff. "Please give Deputy Tom your statement. What's your name?" Sheriff Murphy asked.

"My name is Nancy," she said.

Fire Chief Logan stood up and pulled the sheriff to the side. "She's gone. There isn't anything we can do for her," he said.

The sheriff's face turned red, and he slammed his fist on the table. He curled his lips as anger rose inside of him. He charged at Frank and punched him in the face. Frank fell to the ground, and the sheriff pulled out his billy club and began beating him.

Tom grabbed Mike and sent him to the ground. "Don't you move, you son of a bitch!" Tom yelled.

Frank cried out. "I didn't mean it. I didn't mean to do it. It was an accident." The sheriff kicked him in the groin.

Fire Chief Logan and the two EMTs grabbed the Sheriff and pulled him away.

"How many times have these two bastards gone to jail for beating up on somebody's daughter? How many? Well, Frank, you did it this time. You'll never see the light of day!" the sheriff yelled as he grabbed his hat off the floor.

Frank was still on the floor, curled up in a ball and sobbing. Deputy Tom pulled him to his feet and handcuffed him.

"It was an accident," Frank cried out as Tom was taking him to the car. "You'll get your day in court," Tom said as the EMTs picked up Ashley's lifeless body and put it in the ambulance.

"All right, there is no more to see," the sheriff said, breaking up the crowd. Mike and Tammy ran to their car to follow the ambulance.

Deputy Sam took Frank's picture and fingerprinted him before locking him in his cell.

"I didn't mean to do it. It was an accident," Frank cried. His head was spinning, and his stomach was turning, as he was still drunk from earlier that night.

"Can I make a phone call?" he asked Sam.

"You just get some sleep," the deputy said. "You can make your call in the morning."

"Is Ashley going to be all right?" he asked.

Sam's eyes widened, and he looked at Frank. "She expired, Son," he said, feeling sorry for the guy. "Just lie down and try to get some rest."

Just then, Sheriff Murphy walked up to Frank's cell. "You kids think you can do whatever the hell you want, but we've got you now," he said.

"It was an accident!" Frank yelled.

"Yeah, well tell it to the judge." The sheriff walked out of the room and went upstairs. He walked into his office and called Tom. "We've got to find that son of a bitch Anton before he kills my daughter," he said. "I tried calling her cell phone, but it kept going to voice mail. I told Sam and I told Jerry that Frank, Mike, and Anton are nothing but trouble, but this is my chance to get rid of them once and for all."

"Well, let's go find them," Tom said. "I'm with you 100 percent."

"Frist, I have to get my daughter. Then we'll deal with Anton."

"Let's try the diner," Tom suggested. "Anton always hangs out there."

Chapter 38

ZOE FINISHED TAKING Anton and Taylor's order and walked to the window to give it to Max. Anton reached out his hand so Taylor could hold it while they waited on their food.

"The movie was nice. Thank you, Anton," Taylor said with a smile.

"Thanks. I wanted to take you to Blanco State Park tonight, but I wanted to talk to you about something first," Anton said. His heart was pounding, and his knees were shaking. He took a deep breath to calm his nerves.

Taylor looked at him with concern. Her eyes got wide, and her heart began to pound. She could read the expression on his face and knew he wanted to say something serious.

"Okay. What do you want to talk about?" she asked calmly.

"I was thinking about us and your father and everything that happened. I know that your father kicked you out because of me, but I don't think we are ready to live together. I think I should take you home."

Taylor took a deep breath and then closed her eyes.

Anton's heart sank, and he squeezed her hand. "Don't get me wrong. I love you. I just want to do the right thing. I don't want you fighting with your father because of me. I'm not breaking up with you. We are still going to see each other, but I want you to make up with your father and ask for his forgiveness."

Taylor looked at Anton and held tightly to his hand. "It's okay, Anton. I was thinking the same thing last night. I just didn't know how to tell you. I think I should find my father and go home. It will be best for the both of us."

Anton smiled and leaned over to kiss Taylor. "I still think we should have a meeting with Pastor Andrew," he added. "I called his secretary, and he is supposed to get back to me on Monday. Maybe he could help us talk to your dad."

Zoe brought their food. "Spaghetti and meatballs for you, Anton, and a double cheeseburger for you, Taylor. And two Cokes. Will that be all?" she asked.

"Yes. Thank you, Zoe," Taylor said. "If you need me, I'll be over here." "Thank you," Anton said.

Zoe walked over to the counter and began cleaning it off. The diner was clearing out after a late evening crowd. Only three couples remained, and Zoe had time for a break.

"I talked to Jerry, and he told me that I could be Alex's guess next Sunday in young adult service," Anton noted. "I was thinking that maybe we both could be his guests."

"Of course, I would be glad to go," Taylor said, still smiling. "Although, I'm not sure how that will work given that Alex hates my guts. He's not like his father. Did you know that he and Jonathan came to the garage to jump on me?"

"Alex and Jonathan are cool people," Taylor tried to assure him. "We've been friends practically my whole life. They just thought you wanted to hurt me, but if you get to know them, they can be pretty cool."

"I don't know," Anton said, "but if you say so. I guess I can be nice to them … So how did you like the movie?"

"It was great. I'm glad you share my love for horror movies," Taylor said. "I've wanted to see that movie since it came out. I usually go to the movies with Zoe, but she isn't a fan of horror, and it's no fun going to the movies with my father."

"I enjoyed watching the movie with you too," Anton said with a smile.

*****

Sheriff Murphy and Deputy Tom got out of their squad car and walked up to the diner window. Sheriff Murphy saw Taylor sitting in a booth with Anton. He tapped on the window and then headed inside.

Taylor looked up, and her heart sunk when she saw her father storm through the door. He marched up to Anton and put his hand on his gun. Deputy Tom stood beside him and put his hand on his gun also.

"Taylor, get away from that scum bag!" the sheriff shouted, looking at Anton.

"Daddy, please!" Taylor screamed.

"Taylor, I'm only going to tell you once. Now get up."

"What did I do?!" Anton shouted. "You can't just come in here barking orders. We didn't do anything!"

"Anton, I told you once to stay the hell away from my daughter! You, Frank, and Mike are nothing but scum. You're troublemakers! All you do is go around town and hurt people! You are terrorists, and you need to be stopped. Well, I have had it with your whole bunch. You have two days to get out of town!"

"Get out of town?" Anton questioned. "Why? Because of Taylor?

She is a grown person. She can see whomever the hell she wants to see." The sheriff stepped back and pulled out his gun.

"What are you going to do? Shoot me?" Anton shouted.

"I'm warning you ... Sit down and shut up!" the sheriff said angrily. Taylor jumped up and stood in front of Anton. "Daddy, please. I'm coming ... Put your gun away."

The sheriff looked at Taylor, and he put his gun back in his holster. "Let's go," he said as he grabbed Taylor by the arm. "This isn't over, Anton," the sheriff added as he walked out the door.

Anton's heart was in his throat, and his hands were shaking. He sat down in his seat and put his head in his hands.

Zoe was standing motionless at the counter. She didn't know what to do as she watched the sheriff.

Anton sat shaking in his seat when his phone rang. He looked at the caller ID and saw it was Mike.

"Hello," he said.

"Anton, I was trying to reach you," Mike said. "Why? What's up?" Anton asked.

"It's Frank. He's in trouble."

"What did he do?" Anton asked.

"He killed Ashley at Leo's tonight."

Anton's heart sank, and his head began to spin. "He what?"

"He punched her, and she fell and hit her head on the table. Anton, it's bad. I'm with her mother at the coroner. Where are you?" "I'm at the diner," Anton said.

"Stay there. I should be there in a half an hour," Mike said.

Anton ended the call and looked out the window. He couldn't believe what he'd just heard. He looked down at his plate, but he couldn't finish his meal. He just pushed his plate to the side and rested his head on the table.

Zoe looked at Anton and walked over to him. "Would you like anything else?" she said quietly, feeling sorry for him for the first time.

He looked up at her and shook his head no.

Two girls came in the diner and sat up at the counter. Zoe walked over to wait on them. They were two of the girls who had been at Leo's that night.

"Did you hear what happened tonight at Leo's?" one of the girls asked. "No. What happened?" Zoe asked.

"Frank Mitchell hit Ashley Bell and killed her. She died instantly. The sheriff went off," the girls told Zoe.

Zoe looked over at Anton, and the girl turned around and looked too. "He's usually with those guys. I saw him a couple of times at Leo's," she noted. "It was awful."

"Yeah," Zoe said. "It sounds terrible."

She took their order and placed it in the window.

*****

Taylor sat in the back of the squad car as Tom drove them home. "Taylor, I told you time and time again about Anton and his bunch," the sheriff said. "Did you hear Frank killed Ashley Bell?" "What?!" Taylor asked.

"You heard me. He hit her, and she fell and hit her head. I knew those boys were no good. That could have been you."

"Daddy, Anton would never hit me."

"You don't know that. When you are full of beer, anything can happen, and that's all they do is drink and get plowed."

Taylor sat quietly in the back. She couldn't believe Ashley was dead. She looked out the window at the houses as they drove by—nice little houses that looked like everyone was happy, but who knows what troubles went on behind closed doors.

She thought about Anton and what might have happened if her father would have pulled his trigger. She thought about Frank and how scared he must be right now.

Why do these things happen the way they do? Why can't we just be happy? All Taylor wanted to do was date Anton. She didn't mean to hurt anyone. Now Frank was in jail, Ashley was dead, and her father forbid her to see Anton. It was all a big mess, and she didn't know what to do to fix it. Taylor felt like everything was her fault, even though deep down inside she knew better. Deputy Tom parked in front of their house, and Taylor got out and walked to the door. Her father walked behind her.

"I'll see you tomorrow, Sheriff," Tom said.

The sheriff opened the door, and Taylor walked inside.

Chapter 39

FRANK WAS LYING in his cell curled up on the bed. He was reliving last night over and over again in his mind. His skin crawled, his stomach did flip-flops, and his chest felt tight. He tossed and turned, but he couldn't shake the fear built up inside of him. "Ashley was right. I'm nothing but a coward," he cried.

He closed his eyes and saw Ashley's lifeless body lying on the floor. He jumped, shook his head, and forced back down the vomit rising in his throat. "I'm going to prison. I can't make it in prison. I've never been in jail before," he said. I didn't mean to do it. It was an accident." He repeated the words over and over.

Frank got up and paced in his cell, but he could hear Ashley scream as she hit the floor. He could see the people looking at him, pointing at him. He could hear them laughing. He closed his eyes and could see the sheriff coming at him with the billy club.

A lump grew in his throat. He pulled at his hair. He began to pace faster and faster, but he could still hear Ashley calling him a coward. He began to shake as the fear traveled up and down his spine. He looked out the window of his cell door, but he couldn't see anyone. He was alone. Alone with his thoughts.

I can't go to prison, he thought. *I've never been outside of San Juan. My mother ... What is she going to do when I'm gone?*

The noise in his head was growing louder. He couldn't turn off the scene of seeing himself hit Ashley. He watched her fall to the floor. He looked at the light fixture on the ceiling and then looked at the sheet on the bed.

He looked over in the corner, and he could see Ashley. "Do it. Do it, you coward," he could hear her say.

He grabbed a sheet off the bed and wrapped it up like a long rope.

He stood on the bed and tied one end of the sheet to the light fixture.

"Do it, you coward," he could hear Ashley say.

He tied the other end of the sheet around his neck. He closed his eyes and could see Ashley lying there helplessly on the floor.

"I'm sorry, Ashley," he said. "Mama, I'm sorry."

With that, he jumped off the bed, breaking his neck as he swung back and forth.

*****

Sheriff Murphy poured himself a cup of coffee when Deputy Sam came into the office.

"Sheriff, I heard Taylor was at home," Deputy Sam said. "She is," the sheriff said as he took a sip of coffee.

"How is she?"

"She's doing fine now that she's away from that punk, Anton. I told you that whole bunch—Anton, Frank, and Mike—are nothing but trouble. And now look … A person is dead."

"Sheriff, you can't blame Anton for what Frank did," Sam said. "Anton and Frank are two different people."

"But that's all they do is beat up on women."

"Have you ever heard that Anton ever hit a woman?" Sam questioned. "Anton got into a lot of fights, but not with any women."

The sheriff looked at Sam. "Well, I'm not going to give him a chance to hit Taylor."

"Sheriff, Taylor's been with Anton for two weeks, and they haven't gotten in to any fights so far. You have to give Anton a chance."

The sheriff listened to Sam. He knew that he was right, and he was running out of excuses to continue this fight with Anton. "Okay, Sam … Did you check on our guest?" the sheriff said as he put his feet on his desk and leaned back.

"I was just going to take him some breakfast in a few minutes," Sam said, pouring some coffee in a Styrofoam cup. "He wants to make a phone call." "Let him make his phone call when he gets through eating, Sam," the sheriff said.

Sam took the tray of food downstairs. He took his key and opened the cell door. His eyes widened, and he dropped the tray. He ran to the stairs and called for the sheriff and Tom and then ran back to the cell and grabbed Frank by the waist.

The sheriff ran downstairs, threw his hands in the air, and screamed, "You stupid kid."

Tom looked in cell, and his heart dropped as he saw Sam holding Frank up.

"Tom, untie that sheet," the sheriff said.

Tom ran over and stood on the bed to untie the sheet from the light fixture. Frank collapsed on the floor.

"Call the paramedics," the sheriff said.

"He's gone," Sam said as he closed Frank's eyes. "What are we going to do now?" Sam asked.

"There isn't anything more we can do," the sheriff said.

Within a few minutes, Fire Chief Logan and two EMTs came down the stairs.

"What happened?" Logan asked.

"He hung himself, that stupid kid," the sheriff said.

"Well there isn't anything we can do for him now," Logan said.

"I have to call his next of kin," Sheriff Murphy said, shaking his head. "Do you know who they are?" Logan asked.

"He lives with his mother on the west side of town. I guess Sam and I could go over there."

Sheriff Murphy and Deputy Sam got into the squad car, and Sam drove. The sheriff looked out the window. He thought about Anton and Taylor and what Sam had said about forgiveness. He thought about Frank and how scared he was and how he said he didn't mean to do it.

He hated this part of his job—telling a loved one that someone had passed away. But that was his job, and there was no way around it.

He thought about Taylor and how fragile she was. He didn't want to drive her to suicide. How could he get through to her without hurting her again?

Maybe he could send her away on another long trip to Europe with her aunt. She'd like that. She needed to get away from this town and these crazy kids. He closed his eyes and saw Frank hanging there in his cell, and his heart went out to his family.

How is Taylor going to react when I tell her that another of her friends has died? he wondered. *Two losses within twenty-four hours.* Sheriff Murphy rubbed his face and took a deep breath.

Mrs. Mitchell was an older woman, and he knew she was going to take the news hard. It was bad enough telling her Frank was in jail.

The car turned on Second Street, and the sheriff took another breath as he tried to calm his nerves. Sam parked the car, and they both got out.

They walked slowly up the path and knocked on the door. Mrs. Mitchell came to the door. She looked at the sheriff and then at Sam.

"Mrs. Mitchell, I'm sorry to inform you—" the sheriff said.

"Oh no! My baby!" Mrs. Mitchell shouted before she collapsed onto the floor.

Chapter 40

ANTON CAME IN from work. He looked at his watch and saw it was five fifteen. He walked over to the kitchen and threw his keys on the counter. He then went over to his aquarium and turned on the light.

"Hey, boy," he said. He grabbed his old coffee can, plucked out two worms, and fed Charlie.

He put the coffee can back and headed for the bathroom to wash his hands. He wanted to call Taylor, but first he was going to fix himself something to eat. He walked over to the refrigerator and pulled out some chicken that Taylor had already prepared.

He set the timer on the oven, turned it on, and placed the pan of chicken in the oven. Then he got a bowl of mashed potatoes that Taylor had made and put it in the microwave. He set the timer for two minutes.

He walked in the bedroom, pulled off his work clothes, and put on a pair of shorts and a T-shirt before sliding his feet in a pair of slippers. He walked over to the television and turned it on. The Syfy channel was showing an old episode of *Star Trek*.

He checked the guide and realized they were having a *Star Trek* marathon. He turned the volume up and walked to the kitchen. He checked the chicken, but it wasn't quite hot enough. He turned around, took the bowl of potatoes out of the microwave, and set it on the counter.

Next, he reached in the cabinet and took out a plate. He went to the refrigerator and grabbed a beer. Opening it, he took a swallow. He was pulling the chicken out of the oven when someone began pounding on his front door. He jumped and looked at his door. He walked over to it and yelled, "Who is it?"

"Anton, it's me," Mike said in a high-pitched voice like he had been crying. Anton opened the door, and Mike pushed his way in.

"He's dead, Anton," he cried. "He's dead." "Who is dead?" Anton asked.

"Frank," Mike said.

Anton's heart jumped into his throat. "You're kidding, right? Tell me you're kidding." Anton shook Mike by the shoulders as he spoke.

"No. I saw him myself. His mother called me to go identify the body with her at the morgue."

"What happened?" Anton asked.

"The sheriff said he hung himself in his cell."

Anton's mind went a million miles away. It seemed as if he was floating in space. He could hear Mike talking, but it sounded like he was in another room down the hall. Anton walked over to the couch and flopped down.

"Anton!" Mike called.

Anton sat there with his mouth open. "Anton!"

Anton looked at Mike. "Do you believe he killed himself, or do you think the sheriff and Tom had something to do with it?"

"The coroner said it was a suicide. I could see the marks where he had been hanging from his neck," Mike said. "I don't think the sheriff had anything to do with it."

"Probably not. You and I both know Frank was always kind of nervous," Anton cried. "He couldn't take going to jail."

"He couldn't face the fact that he killed Ashley," Mike said as he wiped at his tears.

"That was an accident," Anton said. "Frank didn't mean to do it."

*****

Taylor rushed home from school. Once inside, she set her books on the kitchen island, went to the refrigerator, and took out a pan with a meatloaf in it. She had prepared it earlier that morning before she went to school.

She placed the pan in the oven and began to peel potatoes. She wanted to make her father a special dinner since he hadn't really had a home-cooked meal since she'd been gone. She washed the potatoes, put them in a pot, and started them to boiling.

She went over to the kitchen counter and turned on the radio. A Katy Perry song was playing, so she turned it up. Her father wasn't going to be home for another hour, so she had the house to herself. Taylor felt happy, because her father had been extra nice to her ever since she'd come home. He hardly mentioned Anton. The house was a mess when she got home, but she didn't mind. She immediately got to work cleaning it up.

Taylor checked the cabinets and the refrigerator and made a list of the things they needed so her father could pick them up on his way home. The potatoes were ready. She poured off the water and got the milk, butter, and potato masher and whipped up the mashed potatoes. She checked the meatloaf. It was almost ready, so she set the plates on the kitchen counter like always and waited for her father to come home. She thought about calling Anton but decided to wait.

Sheriff Murphy walked into the front door and immediately smelled the meatloaf cooking. He was happy that Taylor was home, and he'd enjoyed peace of mind all day. But he worried about how she was going to react when he told her about Frank.

He took the groceries into the kitchen and found Taylor was sitting at the kitchen island. The food was hot and ready to eat. The sheriff wanted to wait until after dinner to tell her about Frank, but he just came out with it.

"Taylor, I have something to tell you," he said in a very serious tone.

Taylor looked up at him, and her heart began to pound.

"Frank killed himself in his cell today."

Taylor's eyes widened. She could hardly believe what she was hearing. "What?" she asked.

"Frank killed himself. He hung himself in his cell with a sheet." Taylor put her head in her hands and began to cry. The sheriff walked over to her and pulled her up into his arms.

"I'm sorry, honey. I'm so sorry about your friends," he said, feeling pity for his daughter. "Mrs. Bell told me that Ashley's funeral is going to be on Wednesday. I'll go with you if you want me to. There is no word yet on Frank's funeral, but when I hear, I'll let you know."

"I cooked your favorite meatloaf," Taylor said, pointing to the food. "I know. Thank you, honey," the sheriff said.

They sat down and began to eat. Taylor wanted to call Anton to see how he was doing after hearing about Frank.

After dinner, the sheriff got up and went into the living room and turned on a baseball game. He sat in his recliner and fell asleep. Taylor cleared the dishes and loaded the dishwasher and then put the food in storage bowls and placed them in the refrigerator.

She grabbed her books and her cell phone and went into her room. She collapsed on her bed and dialed Anton's number.

He picked up the phone on the first ring. "Hello?" "Did you hear?" Taylor asked.

Anton took a deep breath and then he bit his lip. "Yes," he said. "I'm sorry, Anton," Taylor said.

"Frank was my friend—and Ashley too," Anton cried.

"I know," Taylor said. "I'm so sorry that this happened. Do you want to go to Ashley's funeral together?" Taylor asked.

"Yes. We could go together," Anton said.

"My father didn't hear when Frank's funeral was going to be."

"His mother didn't know yet. She might have to cremate him. She didn't have any insurance," Anton said.

Taylor's heart skipped a beat when she heard that. She felt sorry for Mrs. Mitchell. she was alone now that Frank was dead. "I'm sorry to hear that," Taylor said.

"Are you going to be all right, Anton? You don't sound so good." "I'll be all right. I just have to think," he said.

"You want to meet tomorrow?" Taylor asked.

Anton took a deep breath. "After work I can meet for a little while. I have to help Frank's mother get things ready." "Okay, Anton. I'll see you tomorrow."

"See you," Anton said as he ended the call.

Chapter 41

ANTON WAS JUST about through breaking down the cash register and was getting ready to lock the doors to the shop when Deputy Jerry walked in.

"Hey, Jerry. I'll be with you in a second," Anton said. He put on the closed sign and locked the doors.

"You can go to the back," Anton said.

Jerry walked to the break room and sat down. Anton checked the doors in the garage and then came to the break room.

"You want some coffee?" he asked Jerry as he poured himself a cup. "No thank you," Jerry said.

Anton sat down on the opposite side of the table. "How are you holding up, Anton?" Jerry asked.

"I'm getting by. I can't believe Frank would do something like that." "Well, he was really frightened and nervous when we locked him up. I guess he couldn't take it," Jerry said.

"Frank was always a little odd, but I didn't think he would take his own life. He wasn't as outgoing as me and Mike, but I thought he had it together. I mean, he never showed that he could get so depressed that he would commit suicide."

"Well, you have to look at the circumstances. He had just killed Ashley, which could weigh heavily on anyone's mind," Jerry said.

"I guess so."

"Was Ashley his girlfriend?"

"No, she was just a friend. We've hung out together since high school. Are you going to be at the funeral?" Anton asked.

"Yes. The whole town will be there," Jerry said. "How is Taylor getting by?" "She's doing fine. I talked to her last night," Anton said. "The sheriff is still being an asshole. He jumped on me the night Frank killed Ashley. He drew his gun on me right in the middle of the of the diner.

"I don't know what I'm going to do now that all of this has happened. He is really upset and angry. I want to continue to see Taylor, but I don't know how I'm going to make her father see that I'm not that kid anymore," Anton said.

"Why don't you talk to him?" Jerry asked. "Talk to him?" Anton repeated, surprised.

"Yeah. Go to his office, sit down, and have a man-to-man talk with the sheriff. Tell him you really like Taylor, that you want to date her, and that you are not the person you use to be. Tell him you have a nice job, which he knows, and you are planning to go back to school. Tell him everything you told me. Hell, tell him you are even planning to attend church. Be sincere and honest."

"What if he still says no?"

"Well at least you tried, and you know where he stands. That's all you can do. The rest is on him," Jerry said. "But I know the sheriff. He will listen and respect your honesty. He likes that in a man. Before you go to him, pray about it and leave it in God's hands. God will work it out."

Anton listened. He tossed the idea around in his mind. *What harm could it do? I have to give it a shot.* He thought it over. *It's worth a try.*

Anton took a big swallow of coffee and looked at Jerry. "When I go to see the sheriff, would you like to go in the office with me?" he asked.

"Sure. Just wait until after everything blows over and everything calms down, and then talk to him. Sam has been talking to the sheriff, and I think he is getting through to him. Just give it a couple of days until all of this blows over. In the meantime, pray about it and tell Taylor to pray about it as well. Well, I have to be going. I've got to go to the grocery store." Jerry got up and grabbed his hat. "I'll see you later," he said as he walked toward the door.

Anton followed him, and they walked outside together. Jerry went to his car, and Anton locked the doors. He watched Jerry as he drove off before going to his car. He got inside and drove down Main Street, thinking about what Jerry said.

"Talk to the sheriff. Tell him how you feel about Taylor." *Well, it's worth a shot*, he thought.

Anton drove to the park, parked his car, and watched the boys play basketball. He thought about Frank and Mike and how they used to play basketball and bowl. Now it was all over, and things would never be the same.

Frank was gone. Ashley was gone. He thought about Mike and the job he wanted to do with James. Anton knew that was a bad idea. *What if that goes wrong?* He took out his phone and looked at his photos. He looked at a funny picture of Frank falling down at the bowling alley and pulling Ashley down with him. His heart sank.

"They are gone, and things will never be the same," he said as tears formed in his eyes.

Just then, his phone rang, and Anton looked at the caller ID and saw it was Mike.

"Hello, Anton. Where are you?" Mike asked.

"I'm at the park. I had to get some fresh air. Is everything all right?" Anton asked.

"Yes. I just came from Frank's mother's house. The funeral is set for Thursday, right after Ashley's. He's only going to have a memorial service because she is having him cremated."

"I see," Anton said. He took a deep breath. "I'm sorry I didn't go over there. I just couldn't face—" "I know," Mike said.

"You want to meet? I don't want to be alone right now," said Mike.

"Let's go to Roscoe's and hang out."

"All right. Who's driving?" Anton asked. "I'll drive," Mike said.

"Okay. I'll meet you at my place in a half an hour," Anton said. "All right," Mike said before ending the call.

Anton put his phone in his pocket. He laid his head back on his seat and closed his eyes. He took a deep breath and listened to the sounds in the park. He could hear the birds singing and the kids playing. He could hear the cars driving by. He remembered the last time he was at the park with Frank and Mike. He remembered how they enjoyed being together. Frank and Mike were the first two people he met when he got to San Juan. He thought that they were going to be friends forever. He remembered the night they took Tammy and Ashley to Dallas and how they drove around downtown until early the next day. He thought days like that would never end.

Anton sat up and put the car in drive. He slowly drove down the street. He could hear Frank laughing and telling him the scores of the Dallas game. He remembered that he had two tickets to the Dallas versus Green Bay game for next Sunday. He had planned to take Frank. What was he going to do now?

Frank was his partner when he went to sporting events. It had been that way since ninth grade. He remembered when Frank's father took him to his very first football game. It was Dallas versus the Bears. Dallas won, and Anton had been a fan ever since.

Now that Frank was gone, who would be there to fill his shoes? Tears formed in his eyes, and he squeezed the steering wheel to keep from crying. He thought about Taylor and what she might be doing right now. He wanted to call her, but he couldn't bring himself to do it.

Anton wanted to tell her about the pain he was feeling after he'd lost his friends, but Taylor really didn't know Frank—not like he did. She wouldn't understand how he felt. He wanted to be with someone who was experiencing the same pain he was. That's why he was going out with Mike.

I'll call Taylor tomorrow, he thought as he drove down the street. He looked at the people walking and shopping and going about their daily lives, and he wanted to shout out the window that his friends were dead. They were gone. But it seemed as though no one cared. No one but him and Mike.

Chapter 42

JONATHAN FINISHED HIS quiz early and set his paper a side. He looked across the room at Taylor. She was still working on her quiz. He thought about Frank and Ashley and wondered how Taylor was holding up since they were her friends. He knew that Anton must be hurting right now, because Mike and Frank were his boys, and they were inseparable.

He felt bad for Frank and Ashley even though he never really cared for them. Everyone was talking about going to Ashley's funeral. She was a popular girl ever since high school. Jonathan's mother told him to attend the funeral to represent the family.

He took a casserole that his mother had made over to Ashley's mother's house. His father donated some more food from the store. He heard how the sheriff had pulled a gun on Anton the other day, and Taylor stepped in the way.

He didn't even want to imagine what would have happened if the sheriff gun would have gone off. Alex was telling him that his father had been talking to Anton and that he invited him to be a guest at the church and Anton said yes.

Maybe Anton is trying to change. .he thought. *Even so, he's was wrong for her.* He stood up, took his quiz to his instructor, and sat back down. He looked at Taylor, and his heart went out to her. Even though she was with Anton, he still liked her, and he made up his mind to tell her one last time.

The timer went off.

"Okay, people, put down your pencils," Mr. Bookstien said.

Taylor put down her pencil, and Mr. Bookstien walked over and collected the quizzes.

"All right, people, read chapters 22 through 26 for next week. I'll see you then."

Taylor put her book in her book bag and stood up. Jonathan walked over to her.

"Taylor," he asked. "Do you have a moment?"

Taylor looked at him. "I've got to run, Jonathan. I'm meeting Anton in a half an hour."

Jonathan's eyes got wide. "It won't take long," he said.

All the students were leaving the classroom, and Mr. Bookstien had gathered his things and walked out.

Zoe and Alex also walked out, leaving Jonathan and Taylor in the room alone.

"Will you have a seat, please?" Jonathan said, pulling a stool out from under the table.

Taylor sat down and looked at Jonathan as he sat down beside her. "How are you holding up>?" he said, concerned for her.

"I'm fine. I just feel bad for Anton. They were really his friends. I tried to let Anton know that I was there for him, but he kind of closed down and shut me out. I don't know if he's still angry with my father, or if he's really hurt over Frank and Ashley."

"Maybe he doesn't want you to see him hurt. Give him a little time to sort things out. He'll come around. Well, he called me earlier today and wanted to meet me after class, so I guess we'll talk then."

Jonathan listened to Taylor, and he realized she was serious about Anton. So he chickened out on telling her his feelings once again. "Taylor, I just wanted to tell you how sorry I am about all that has happened. All I wanted to do was warn you about Anton, Frank, and Mike. I didn't want anyone to get hurt."

"That's okay, Jonathan. None of this was your fault. I appreciate you looking out for me. It's just that I'm with Anton now, I really love him, Jonathan. If it were another—" "I know," Jonathan said sadly.

"Oh, Jonathan. I don't want to lose your friendship, it means the world to me,"

"You won't. You mean the world to me too," Jonathan said, forcing a smile. "Are you going to Ashley's funeral?" Taylor asked.

"Yes. My mother asked me to go," Jonathan said. "The whole town is going to be there,"

"I wish that things were different. Sometimes it feels like it was my fault, Jonathan," Taylor said.

"Don't think that way. Frank was destructive … It was just a matter of time. I just hope for your sake, Taylor, that this incident opened Anton's eyes."

Taylor's eyes grew wide, and a soundlessness came over her. Jonathan looked at Taylor and noticed the change in her.

"I'm sorry, Taylor. Just be careful and watch out for yourself."

"I will, Jonathan. You have to get to know Anton, and you will see that he has really changed and treats me like a queen. He's a real gentleman."

"Of course he is," Jonathan said, forcing a smile. "Well, I have to go. I'm meeting Anton at five thirty."

"Okay, I don't want to hold you up any longer," Jonathan said. He stood up and watched Taylor gather her things. She leaned over and kissed him on the cheek.

"I'll see you later," she said.

"See you around," Jonathan said with a smile.

Taylor got up and walked out of the door. Alex was standing on the other side of the hall when Taylor walked by. He slowly walked back into the biology room.

"What gives?" he said to Jonathan, who was now looking out of the window. He looked down at the row of cars in the parking lot and the students rushing to get into their cars.

"Maybe this is for the best. It wasn't for us to be together," Jonathan said, feeling the lump in his throat. "I tried Alex, but she still wants that jerk Anton."

"What did she say?" Alex asked, feeling sorry for his friend. "Let's be friends," she said. "She wanted to be my friend."

Alex looked at Jonathan when he said the dreaded "let's be friends," the words no man wants to hear. He walked over and put his hand on Jonathan's shoulder.

"I'm sorry, Jonathan. Forget about her," Alex said. "You're right. It just wasn't in the cards. Maybe in another life,"

"Yes, in another life," Jonathan said as he looked at Alex.

"You want to go to Roscoe's? There are some hot girls there—you might get lucky," Alex said, smiling.

"Okay, but you drive. I have to get my rest, so I can look good for the ladies," Anton noted.

"You look good already. It's Taylor's loss, man," Alex said.

Jonathan walked over to the lab table and grabbed his book. "This was a crazy week," he said to Alex.

"I know," Alex said as they walked out the door and down the hall.

"I can't wait until this semester is over, and we have graduation," Jonathan said.

"My father is buying me a new car," Alex said.

"That's great," Jonathan said.

Chapter 43

SAN JUAN COMMUNITY Baptist Church had begun to fill up with friends, family, and other townspeople who were curious and wanted to see what was going on. Sheriff Murphy and Taylor walked into the church sanctuary and looked for a seat. Sheriff Murphy saw Deputy Sam and Deputy Jerry sitting in the back by the entrance, so he told Taylor that he was going to sit with them.

Taylor spotted Anton sitting in a pew behind the family, so she went over and sat by him and Mike.

"I'm glad you made it," Anton whispered. "I came here with the family. That's why I didn't pick you up,"

"That's okay. My father wanted to bring me anyway. He's in the back sitting by Jerry."

Anton turned around and saw the sheriff and a row of law enforcement and firemen sitting in the back. Taylor looked around and saw Jonathan and Alex sitting in the next aisle opposite of her. She looked around but didn't see Zoe.

Mrs. Smith and Mrs. Johnson came in and sat down behind Taylor. "It looks so nice," Mrs. Johnson said. "The casket really looks beautiful."

Taylor looked over at the altar at Ashley's powder-blue casket, and her mind went back to her mother's casket, which had been made the same way—steel with the Lord's Prayer printed around the handle. People were walking up to Mr. and Mrs. Bell and hugging them and giving them their condolences. Mrs. Bell wiped at her nose with a tissue as she sat there and watched the people come in.

Tammy entered the church, walked up to the casket, kissed her hand, and laid it on the casket. Then she turned and walked over to Mrs. Bell and hugged her. She looked at Mike and Anton and straightened up her clothes, looked straight ahead, and walked to the back. Mike jump and dropped his head. Taylor watched Tammy go to the back.

"What's going on with Tammy?" Taylor asked Anton.

Anton squeezed her hand and looked back at Tammy. "I don't know," he said. "We haven't spoken since the incident, and Mike isn't telling me anything."

Mike put his head in his hands and began to cry. The church was growing crowded, and the choir stood up and sang the hymn "Nothing but the Blood of Jesus."

Mrs. Bell let out a cry when the choir began to sing. Anton patted her on the back as tears formed in his eyes. Taylor wanted to excuse herself, but she sat there and watched.

"This is sad. I feel awful for Mrs. Bell," Mrs. Johnson whispered to Mrs. Smith.

"Yeah. We'll have to invite her to lunch one of these days, but I must say that everything is so beautiful," Mrs. Smith said.

"Yes. The flowers that drape the casket and the funeral wreaths are gorgeous," said Mrs. Johnson.

Zoe tiptoed into the sanctuary and looked around for a seat. She saw a spot next to Jonathan, so she tiptoed over to him and sat down. Taylor looked over and gave her a little wave. Anton wiped at the tears in his eyes.

After the burial, they went back to the church for the reception. Taylor rode in the car with her father going to and from the cemetery. People gathered in the dining hall to eat. There was a large buffet on a long table in the back of the hall.

The whole town pitched in to help. That was what the town was good for. They loved to gather together no matter what the occasion. Taylor and Sheriff Murphy entered the dining hall, and Sheriff Murphy went to sit by Sam. Taylor found Anton, who was talking to Jerry.

"How are you holding up?" Jerry asked Anton.

"I'm doing better than I expected," Anton answered. "Everything was nice."

"Yes, it was."

"I'm glad everyone came out," Anton said.

"Yes, they did," Jerry said. He then looked at Taylor. "Taylor, are you going to young adult service with Anton on Sunday?"

"Yes, I'll be here, Deputy. I'm looking forward to it," she told him.

"I'm glad. I want to see you both here." Jerry smiled.

"We'll be here," Anton said, returning the smile.

Zoe and Jonathan were sitting down with their plates of food. "You want to sit by Jonathan and Alex, Anton?" Taylor asked. Anton look over at Jonathan then said, "I guess so."

The pair grabbed their plates and went to sit by Jonathan and Alex. Anton looked at Jonathan, who looked back at him.

"Thanks for coming," Anton said as he reached out his hand for Jonathan to shake it.

"You're welcome," Jonathan said. "Anytime," said Alex.

Mike walked into the church dining hall and looked around for Tammy. She was talking to Mrs. Bell and Patricia, Ashley's little sister. Mike took a deep breath and walked up to Tammy.

"Excuse me, Mrs. Bell," he said as he grabbed Tammy by the arm. "Tammy, I have to talk to you for a second."

They walked out of the exit and down the street to Mike's car. Tammy got in the car, and Mike got into the driver's seat. He looked at Tammy. "Are you sure?!" he yelled.

Tammy began to cry. "Don't yell at me!" she yelled back. "I tested myself three times ... I'm sure."

Mike hit the dashboard. "Well, how do you know it's mine?" he yelled. "Don't do that. Don't you dare. You know it's yours. You are the only person I've been with."

"Well, what are you going to do about it?" Mike asked. "What do you mean *you*? *We* are going to have it."

Mike looked at her and shook his head. "No, I can't. I'm not ready for this."

"Well, you should have thought about it before we did it," Tammy snapped. "I thought that you were using protection?" Mike questioned. "I was, but it's not 100 percent."

Mike hit the dashboard and grabbed the steering wheel. "I had plans, Tammy, and they didn't include you."

Tammy started to cry again. "I can take care of myself, but I'm going to have this baby whether you're there or not."

"Well don't count on me ... Do what you have to do," Mike yelled.

"I will. You just do what you do best—leave," Tammy yelled as she got out of the car.

*****

Anton, Jonathan, and Alex were having a good time talking about the Dallas game against Atlanta. It was a blowout, and Dallas beat Atlanta twenty-eight to seven, and Alex had been there to see the whole thing. Anton told them he had a motorboat on the lake at Blanco State Park and maybe one day they could go fishing.

Jonathan smiled. *He's not such a bad person once you talk to him*, he thought. *He actually has a sense of humor.*

Zoe and Taylor sat and listened as the guys went on and on about football. They tried to join in, but they didn't have much to say, because they didn't know a thing about football. Mike came into the dining hall and went and sat by Anton.

"Mike, tell them about the Green Bay versus Dallas playoff game ... Mike went to the game," Anton noted.

Mike laughed. "There was this one Packers fan in the stands—he had his Packers jersey on—and he kept calling Tony Romo bad names. So this guy in a Cowboys jersey poured a glass of beer on his head. Everyone laughed, and they chased him out of the stadium."

Alex and Jonathan laughed as Mike told his story. Tammy came in and sat back down by Patricia and began to talk. Mike got up and went over to her and pulled her to her feet.

"I'm sorry for what I said," he said. "Whatever you want to do or whatever you need, I'm here for you." "Thank you," she said.

Chapter 44

THE WEATHER WAS pleasant. It was a change from the heat wave that had engulfed the town for two weeks straight. A cool breeze was in the air, and Sheriff Murphy thought it was a perfect day for fishing. He had asked Sam and Jerry to go with him to Blanco State Park that afternoon after work. He hadn't been fishing all summer because he was busy with work, but it was a perfect day, and he didn't want to waste it.

"There isn't a cloud in the sky," the sheriff said as he drove to the diner. He looked around and noticed that everyone was taking advantage of the nice weather. Main Street was crowded, and the little shops were filled with excited customers. Sheriff Murphy parked his car and went into the diner. Maria met him at the door.

"I'm supposed to meet Deputy Sam here," he said.

"This way, Sheriff," Maria said. She took him to the back where Deputy Sam and Deputy Jerry were already settled and looking at their menus. "Hi, Sheriff," Deputy Sam said as Sheriff Murphy sat down.

Maria handed him a menu.

"Will you give us a second?" Jerry asked.

"Sure. I'll be right back," Maria said with a smile.

"It's a nice day today, isn't it, fellows?" The sheriff smiled. Sam looked at him. "You are in a good mood today, Sheriff."

"Well, I feel great … I got a good night rest, the day went well, and I feel good."

Jerry laughed.

"Yeah, today is a good day considering all that's happened in the past week," Sam said.

"Yeah, well, Ashley's memorial service was nice, and Frank is being laid to rest today. Everything is getting back to normal," the sheriff said, still smiling.

"Normal, Sheriff ... So how are things between you and Taylor?" Jerry asked.

The sheriff looked down. "Well, she's back at home. It's going to take some time, but she will see things my way."

"Sheriff, why don't you give Anton a chance. You see that he is trying ... You can't keep up this fight forever," Jerry said.

The sheriff listened to Jerry and thought about how gentle Anton had been with Taylor at the funeral. He noticed how well he was getting along with Jonathan and Alex too. He saw how the whole town came out to support Ashley's family, and they were giving that support to Frank's mom too. He knew they would do the same thing for Anton's mother.

So why are you holding a grudge? he thought. *Taylor is a smart girl. Sam is right. I should trust that Taylor will use the good, sound judgment I taught her. She knows the difference between right and wrong, and if Anton gets out of line, I'll be there to handle him.*

Just then, Maria came back to the table. "Are you ready to order?" she asked.

"Yes," Sam said. "I'll have the skillet stir-fry." "And I'll have the pancake special," Jerry said. "Me too," added the sheriff.

"Okay, coming right up," Maria said as she walked to the front to put in their order.

Every table in the diner was taken, and everyone was talking and laughing and having a good time. The atmosphere went perfectly with the weather and the day the sheriff was having. He enjoyed watching the people take advantage of the day.

Now if only the afternoon would go just as well, it will be a perfect day, he thought. "Are you guys still up for fishing?" he asked.

"You know it, Sheriff. I was ready for this all week," Sam said.

"Yeah, I can't wait to go out there on that boat," Jerry said.

"Good, because I don't know when we will have another chance," the sheriff said.

"Next time, I want to take my son, Alex along. We really haven't spent much time together since he's been at attending college," Jerry said.

"I know. I used to take Taylor fishing all the time, but now we are both busy with her work and school, and me with my duties. I haven't really sat down and talk to her," the sheriff said, beginning to feel bad. "I guess that's what I'm going to do—sit down and talk to Taylor about this whole thing, I'm going to listen and try to understand why she chose Anton. I'm going to ask her why Anton, and maybe she can make me understand, because I don't right now. But I'm tired of fighting with her. You are right, Sam. I don't want to chase her away. I want to listen and understand."

"That's all I've been asking you to do, Daniel. You just need to talk to her and listen. Give her the chance to explain why she wants to be with Anton, and when she gives you her answer, you have to accept it no matter how childish you might think it is," Sam said.

The sheriff rubbed his hand through his hair and took a deep breath. "I will," he said seriously. "I'll accept what she has to say, but she has to have a reason. I taught her to use good judgment and common sense, so I want to know if she is using it."

A few moments later, Maria came back with their food. The sheriff ate his pancakes and looked out the window at the sunny day. *No matter what they say about Anton or Taylor, it's not going to ruin my day*, he thought. *The day is too perfect to waste it thinking about Anton.* The pancakes were perfect to go with the perfect day.

Sam looked at the sheriff, and he knew that he had gone through some kind of change. Was it because of what happened at the station with Frank? Or was it because of Ashley? He didn't know, but he was happy to hear that the sheriff was finally making sense and coming around to see things the way they did. Now they just had to get him to meet with Anton.

Chapter 45

THE SHERIFF GRABBED a cart from the parking lot at the grocery store and pushed it inside the entrance. He noticed that the air-conditioning was on full blasts, but they really didn't need it on such a gorgeous day.

He pushed his cart to the bakery and grabbed that Italian white bread that he and Taylor liked so much. He then went to the butcher's counter and selected two big porterhouse steaks to cook on the grill. Next, he went to produce and found the biggest, prettiest baking potatoes for Taylor to bake in the oven.

He'd enjoyed a perfect day yesterday. He spent the whole afternoon fishing with his friends, and the great feeling he'd had all day yesterday spilled over to today. Everything was going great. Taylor was back, there weren't any big problems at work, and the weather was great. Everything was excellent.

Next, Sheriff Murphy picked a head of lettuce and some tomatoes for a tossed salad. Now all he needed was some salad dressing. He was a ranch man and always would be, but Taylor like blue cheese, so he pushed his cart to the salad dressing aisle.

He stopped on the way and grabbed a bag of coals. He liked to put coals in his gas grill to give his meat that charcoal taste. He also stopped and grabbed a case of cola for Taylor. He was happy that Taylor was back home. Everything had gotten back to normal after the funerals.

He pushed his cart to the salad dressing aisle and began looking for the blue cheese dressing when he heard Mrs. Smith talking. He looked over to the next aisle, and Mrs. Smith and Mrs. Johnson were standing there gossiping again.

"It was nicer than I expected," Mrs. Smith said. "The whole thing was nice, and everyone in town brought something."

"They had a lot of food, Gloria." Mrs. Johnson said.

"The food was nice, and the flowers ... She had the prettiest flowers," Mrs. Smith said.

"Mm-hmm," Mrs. Johnson said, making fun.

"Oh, did you see Taylor? She looked nice the other day as well," Mrs. Smith said with a smile.

"I was surprised. At least she didn't look like a slut like she has been lately," Mrs. Johnson said laughing.

"She stayed around Anton and Mike. I watched her father ... He didn't cause a scene," Mrs. Smith said.

"I know," Mrs. Johnson said. "Did you hear what happened last Saturday night? He pulled his gun on Anton ... said he was going to shoot him."

The sheriff pressed his lips together and tightened his fists as anger grew inside of him.

"I know. Taylor stood in the way of that gun. If it would have gone off, you know where she would be right now," Mrs. Smith said.

"Girl, I don't want to think about it ... Two tragedies are enough for one month."

The sheriff grabbed his cart, put the blue cheese in it, and pushed it to checkout. He thought about his beer and turned around and went to get a case. Mrs. Smith and Mrs. Johnson went to checkout. After they went through the line, they slowly went to the exit.

"You know that Mike and Tammy were acting kind of funny at the funeral," Mrs. Johnson said.

"Yes, I did notice them, but I was watching Taylor and how she hung onto Anton," Mrs. Smith replied.

The sheriff went through checkout and pushed his cart through the exit. He saw Mrs. Johnson and Mrs. Smith standing by the exit still gossiping. He pushed his cart up to them.

"Hi, ladies," he said.

"Oh, hi, Sheriff!" they said together, surprised to see him.

"You know, today is a nice day, but the grocery store is no place for your gossip. You two heckle and talk like free-flowing diarrhea. If you do not break up this meeting, I'm going to haul you both in for loitering. Do you understand me?"

Mrs. Smith's eyes widened, and Mrs. Johnson grabbed her bag.

"Well, I'll see you, Mrs. Smith," Mrs. Johnson said as she began to walk to her car.

"I'll see you, Mrs. Johnson," Mrs. Smith said as she walked out into the parking lot.

The sheriff grabbed his cart and pushed it to his car. He smiled as he put his groceries in the trunk. He looked up and saw little Timmy Armstrong collecting carts.

"Hey, Tim!" he called. Tim came over to his car.

"How are things going, Son?" he asked.

"Things are going great, Sheriff. I just have to work a few short weeks, and then I can buy myself that Xbox I've always wanted."

"That's great, Tim. Keep up the good work."

Sheriff Murphy got into his car and drove down Main Street. He thought about Mrs. Smith and Mrs. Johnson. *If it weren't for Mrs. Smith, I wouldn't have kicked Taylor out. I have to stop being so sensitive. Things are not as bad as I thought they were going to be.*

Taylor is alive, and she's with me, and I'm not going to jump to conclusions anymore, he thought. He turned down Bell and slowly looked at the house on his way home. *Taylor should be home from school by now. She'll be happy that I'm going to grill some steaks tonight.* He was going to invite Tom over, but he wanted to spend this time with Taylor.

He wanted to talk to her about Anton like he told Sam. He wanted to let her know that no matter what, he was going to be there for her, because he was her father. He turned down First Avenue and then down Pine.

He parked in front of the house and looked. He saw Taylor's car parked across the street, and he was relieved she was home. He got out of his car and went around to the trunk when the front door opened to the house.

Taylor came out. "Do you want me to help you bring the groceries in?" she asked, a smiling stretched across her face.

The sheriff smiled back. "You can grab this bag. I thought we might have steaks tonight," he said.

"That's great," Taylor said as she grabbed the bag. "Did you get any dessert?" "I got your favorite ice cream—chocolate chip." "I'm glad," Taylor said.

Chapter 46

MIKE HAD THIRTY minutes to go before his shift was over. He was typing the last of the information from his last call in the computer. It was three o'clock, and on Fridays, three o'clock was the busiest time of the day.

His phone lit up, and the call popped up on the screen. He checked his headset and pressed the button for the call.

"Val-tech Industry. This is Mike speaking. How may I help you?"

"I bought your seven-inch touchscreen tablet, but when I touch it, it won't move from screen to screen," the man's voice on the other in of the phones said.

"It's a double-touch. You have to touch it twice," Mike explained.

"I tried that, but it won't work!" the man yelled. "I touched it twice, three times, but it won't work!"

"I'm sorry for your inconvenience. Let me transfer you to technical support." "You do that!"

"Will you stay on the line until I transfer you?" Mike asked politely.

"Yes!" the man yelled.

"Technical support. This is Trish."

"Hello, Trish. This is Mike. I have someone on the line who is having trouble with our seven-inch tablet. Would you like me to connect you?" "Please go ahead," Trish said.

"Hello, sir," Mike said. "I have Trish on the line from technical support … Thank you, and have a nice day."

Mike transferred the call. "Asshole," he said under his breath as he took off his headset. He looked across the way, and his heart sank. It was Frank's cubicle. Personnel hadn't filled the position yet. Mike turned off his computer and picked up his leather book bag. He reached inside and pull out some army brochures.

"If things don't work out with James, I think I'm going to join the army," he quietly said to himself as he looked at the brochures.

There was a number on the back of one of the brochures. He grabbed his cell phone and dialed the number.

"Army recruiting. This is Sergeant Jones."

"Hello. My name is Mike, and I was thinking about the military," he said nervously.

"How old are you?" the sergeant asked. "I'm twenty-five, sir." "How much education do you have?" "I have some college." "Would you like to come in so we could talk?" the sergeant asked.

"Uh, when?" Mike questioned.

"How about Monday?"

"I have to work Monday, but I get off at three thirty." "Well how about four o'clock?"

"Four sounds good."

"Well, I'll see you Monday at four o'clock." "Okay. Bye," Mike said.

"Goodbye." Mike hung up and then got up and took a deep breath. "I have to do something. I don't want to work at this place all of my life. Besides, I need the benefits for Tammy and the baby."

He looked at the clock on the wall and stood up and walked to the time clock to punch out.

"Mike, are you leaving?" Mike's supervisor, Mrs. Hall asked. "We need you to stay at least until five o'clock. We are short since Frank ..."

"I'm sorry, Mrs. Hall, but I have an emergency." "Okay, but can you come in tomorrow?"

"Only for a few hours," Mike said, punching out. He hurried out of the building and into the parking lot.

*****

Anton had just come in and threw his keys on the kitchen counter. Taylor was coming over at six, and it was his time to cook. He had bought two big pork chops and a bag of frozen French string beans. He placed the chops in a pan, seasoned them with salt and pepper, and place them under the broiler. Next, he put the beans in a pot and added a little water and started them to steaming.

He took an apple pie out of the box and placed it in the middle of the table and then hurried to the bedroom and changed out of his work clothes, throwing on a T-shirt and some jeans. He came out and check the food. The beans were done, so he turned them off and set them aside.

The pork chops still had a while, so he went over and turned on the television. He flipped through the channels before settling on the news. He turned up the sound and looked around to see if everything was in order.

His gym shoes were lying on the floor in front of the couch, so he went and picked them up and tossed them in the closet. The pork chops were beginning to smell good, but they still need a little more time. Anton sat down and began watching the news. When his doorbell rang, he stood up and walked to the door. He peeked through the peep hole and saw it was Mike. His heart sank, because Frank wasn't with him.

He opened the door, and they shook hands and hugged.

"What's going on?" Anton asked as Mike came through the door. "The same old thing. It feels strange at work without Frank. His cubicle is still empty. Everything is backed up, and my supervisors are begging people to stay overtime. No one wants to stay."

"I feel for you," Anton said. "Every time the bell rings I expect to see Frank at the door. It's hard, and it's sad to know he's never coming back." "I know ... What are you doing? It smells good in here," Mike said. "I'm making a little something for Taylor," Anton responded.

"You're having her over tonight? Do you want me to come back?" "No. You can stay. She won't be here until six."

Mike sat on the couch. Anton went over to the stove and pulled out the pork chops, put them on a plate, and set them on the table like Taylor did for him. Mike hesitated and then he took a deep breath.

"Did you think about it some more, Anton?" he asked.

"Think about what?" Anton asked, confused.

"You know ... the job with James?"

Anton frowned and then shook his head no. "Mike, after everything that happened, you're still thinking about that suicide mission?"

"We have it all planned out," Mike said. "I promise you … No one will get hurt."

"You can't make that kind of promise. It just sounds like a bad idea. I don't want to do it, so don't ask me anymore."

"What do you want me to tell James?" Mike asked, frightened.

"Tell him whatever you like. Tell him I'm not interested, and I'm not going to do it."

Mike knew when Anton was serious about something, so he didn't press any longer. He just changed the subject. "I was talking to an army recruiter today," Mike said.

Anton's eyes widened. "Why?" he asked.

"I was thinking about joining. I need the benefits. Tammy is pregnant, and I'm in a dead-end job. I have to do something to get my life together," Mike said.

"Do you think you could do that in the army?" Anton asked.

"Well, I've been thinking about it for a while now, and after Frank died, I guess I've been thinking about it even more. My dad thinks it's a good idea."

"Well, if you think that it's going to help you, anything is better than that idea you had with James," Anton said. "You'll have great benefits, you can see the world, and when you get out, you will be a veteran. You should do it, Mike."

"I think I will. What about you?" Mike asked.

"I'm taking some classes at the university," Anton told him. "I talked to an admissions counselor, and I'm going to take some spring courses. They took my sixty credit hours from Lincoln College, so when I start, I'll be a junior."

"What are you going to major in?"

"I was thinking about biology. I want to be a veterinarian after I graduate. I'm going to attend Texas A&M School of Veterinary Medicine, and I'll continue to work at the garage until I graduate," Anton said.

"Well, once I get in the army, I can use my GI Bill and go back to school too," Mike said.

Chapter 47

SHERIFF MURPHY HAD just sat down to watch the Astros in the pennant race. It was the first game, and he was excited. The Astros had a near-perfect year—the best record in baseball this year. Only the Red Sox matched them in wins. Now they would face off in the American League championship.

Sheriff Murphy had his snacks and beer ready. He had just eaten a terrific dinner that Taylor had cooked, and now it was time for baseball. He had waited all year for this moment. He had bet Tom that the Astros would make it this far, and they did. Tom was a Rangers fan, but the Astros knocked them out of the playoffs.

The Astros were at home, so the Red Sox were up at bat. They had two outs and a man on second.

"Come on!" the sheriff yelled as the batter swung and missed. "That's right … Throw another pitch just like that one."

The pitcher threw the ball, and the batter fouled it off. The sheriff was beginning to sweat, and butterflies filled his stomach. The batter fouled off again.

"Come on … Get him," the sheriff yelled. He took a swallow of beer and muttered a little prayer. "Strike him out!"

The batter swung and missed. "Strike three," the umpire called.

The sheriff jumped up and clapped. "We've got this game," he said as he sat back down.

The television went to a commercial, and the sheriff leaned back in his chair. He began to relax as his stomach began to settle.

I get too worked up. It's only a game, although a very important game, he thought.

*****

Taylor had finished putting the food away in the refrigerator, and she started the dishwasher. She went in her room and closed the door. She wanted to talk to her father about Anton. Her father had been extra nice for the past week, and when she went out with Anton the other night, he didn't make a fuss. She wanted to tell him that they were going to young adult service on Sunday, but she was afraid that he was going to start yelling.

She wanted to date Anton, but she didn't want to feel like she had to sneak around. She wanted her father's blessing. She wanted her father to accept Anton. She had done what Jerry asked her to do. She prayed long and hard about the situation.

Now she just wanted to talk to her father. She wanted to ask him that night, because tomorrow was Saturday, and she would only have one more day until Sunday. She peeked out the door and heard her father cheering on the Astros.

She decided to wait. She sat on her bed and picked up her biology book. She thumbed through the pages, but something kept telling her to go in there and talk to her father.

Oh, Lord, if this is you nudging me, please make everything all right. She prayed as she stood up and walked to the door. She slowly opened the door and walked down the hall to the dining room. She could see her father sitting in his recliner, so she took a deep breath and marched into the living room.

The sheriff looked up at Taylor when she came in the living room. "What's wrong?" he asked as Taylor stood in front of the television. "Daddy, could I talk to you?" Taylor asked nervously.

The sheriff looked at her. He knew what she wanted to talk about. He nodded and turned off the television. "Go ahead," he said as he sat up in his recliner.

A lump rose in Taylor's throat, because she thought her father was going to yell. "Pastor Andrews has invited me and Anton to young adult service on Sunday night. We are going to be Alex Monroe's guests. You know Alex, Deputy Jerry's son."

The sheriff looked at Taylor, and it seemed like an eternity before he responded.

"Taylor, why did you choose Anton out of all the boys in San Juan?" the sheriff asked, curious.

Taylor's eyes widened, and she took a deep breath. She didn't have to think about this answer, because she knew. It was what she had been telling Zoe, and it was what she had wanted to tell her father since the beginning. "Because when I look at Anton, I see that he is special to me. I can see the good in him when no one else can. When we are together, he talks to me and tells me his dreams, and he only wants to make his life better like all of us, like Jonathan and Alex. He treats me good, and he listens to me. When I need someone to talk to, he is there. I now realize I can depend on him, and he will never let me down. He is my friend," Taylor said, wiping at the tears in her eyes.

The sheriff looked at her, and for the first time, he understood. He knew how she felt, because he'd had the same feelings for Mary when they'd first gotten together. He felt sorry that it took him so long to understand.

He had told Sam that she needed a reason, and it seemed to him that her reason would stand up in court. He smiled at her and stood up. "Come here," he said.

Taylor walked over to him, and he hugged her.

"I understand how you feel, Taylor. I've been where you are now, and if you want to date Anton, I'm not going to stand in your way. As long as he respects you and treats you right, I have nothing more to say. And when he sees me, he needs to treat me with respect and respect my house. We'll get along fine."

Taylor's heart leaped with joy, and a feeling of relief came over her. She couldn't believe her ears. Was she dreaming? She wiped at the tears in her eyes and smiled.

"He will respect me, Daddy, and he will respect you too. You'll see. You will be proud of us. Anton can be a real gentleman at times. He will take care of me. We will date, and we won't cause any trouble, and we won't embarrass you."

"I know, Taylor. You are a grown-up now, and I know you will use good judgment and common sense. I trust you."

Taylor hugged her father went back to her room. "He gave me his blessing. I can see Anton without being ashamed," she said with a smile.

Chapter 48

SHERIFF MURPHY HAD pulled the Eddie Fisher file from the file cabinet. He wanted to go over the report he'd written, because he was to appear in court later that day. The sheriff had to testify, so he wanted to familiarize himself with the case once more.

He read over the report and became angry all over again, because it had been his friend's granddaughter in the car that Eddie had hit.

Just then, Sam walked into the office. "Sheriff, you wanted to see me?" he asked. "Sheriff, are you all right?"

"I'm fine," the sheriff said. "I was just going over the Eddie Fisher case." "I see … Did you want to see me?"

"Yes. I want you to go with me to Mrs. Scott's house. Gloria says she keeps calling 911."

"It's probably nothing, Sheriff. Her cat is probably missing again," Sam said.

"I want to be sure. She's an old lady," the sheriff said. "I called her daughter too. She is supposed to be coming out to see her mother."

"You know how these kids are today. They think only of themselves. They have no time for their parents," Sam said.

"I talked to Taylor last night. She told me that she wanted to go to young adult service with Anton. I did what I told you I was going to do, and she gave me a strong answer. I can accept her honesty, and I gave her my blessing. She was happy."

"I'm glad, Sheriff," Sam said. "Anton is a nice boy. You shouldn't worry.

Taylor knows how to handle herself."

"I hope so. I don't want to have to shoot him, and you know I will." the sheriff said laughing.

"I don't think it will come to that. Anton seems to have his life together," said Sam.

*****

Anton had parked outside the sheriff's office. His knees were shaking, and his stomach was doing flip-flops. A lump rose in his throat, and he took a deep breath and began to breathe in and out. He felt like he was going to throw up and maybe suffocate.

"Be cool … He is just a man." he said to himself. "All he can say is yes or no."

Anton had rehearsed what he was going to say to Sheriff Murphy for two days. He wanted to date Taylor, but he didn't want to ask her father. He didn't want to ask the sheriff for anything, but Jerry said it was the right thing to do.

He wanted to tell the sheriff that he was no longer that out of control boy who first came to San Juan. He had grown up considerably, and he was trying to get his life together. He had his school schedule with him, because he wanted to show the sheriff that he was enrolled in the universe and only had two years to go before he graduated.

He knew the sheriff already knew he had a trade. He was a skilled mechanic and had been for five years. He hadn't been in trouble since he'd gotten out of jail.

"Jail. I've been in jail. The sheriff put me there. He isn't going to let me date Taylor," he said.

Anton put the keys in the ignition and then looked out the window. "Don't chicken out. Just go in there and get it over with. No harm can come to you," he told himself. He turned off the ignition, got out of the car, and walked slowly through the doors.

Anton walked into the deputy's office, and Jerry met him at the desk. "He's in his office, Anton," Jerry said.

"If he's busy, I'll come back," Anton said.

"No, he isn't busy. He would see you," Jerry said.

Anton took a deep breath. "You look worried," Jerry said.

"I am a little nervous," Anton said, rubbing his hand through his hair. Deputy Tom jumped when he saw Anton. He went over to his desk and sat down. Anton looked at Deputy Tom, and his heart jumped into his stomach. Deputy Jerry turned around and looked at Deputy Tom.

"Don't mind him. You didn't come to see him. You came to speak to the sheriff. It's between you and the sheriff." Anton nodded.

"Are you ready?" Jerry asked.

"Give me a second," Anton said. He went to the door and took a deep breath. "Calm down," he said, trying to ease his nerves. "He is only a man."

Deputy Jerry walked over to him. "You want to talk about it?"

"It's just that I don't want to get into a fight. I don't want to make the sheriff angry."

"He won't get angry. I've known the sheriff for a long time. He will respect you more if you come to him like a man. He will listen to you, and he will be fair."

"Will you come in the office with me, Jerry?" Anton asked. "I will," Jerry agreed, "but you have to ask him yourself."

"I know. I just need a second to gather my thoughts." Anton took another breath as he closed his eyes. He opened them back up and turned to Jerry. "All right. I'm ready." He walked behind the desk and into the sheriff's office.

Deputy Jerry knocked on the sheriff's door. "Sheriff, you have a visitor," he said.

The sheriff looked up, and to his amazement, it was Anton. "May I come in, Sheriff?" Anton asked.

The sheriff motioned for Anton to come in.

Anton hesitated and then took a deep breath and walked in. "Sheriff, I wanted to ask you if I could date your daughter?" he asked as he looked the sheriff in the eye.

The sheriff looked at Jerry, then at Sam, and then back at Anton. He thought about what Taylor had said last night and knew he couldn't go back on his word. So he asked Anton the same question he asked Taylor. "Why do you want to date my daughter, Anton?" he asked.

Anton's heart pounded, and he took a moment before he spoke. "I knew a lot of girls in town before I knew Taylor, but Taylor is different.

She is not like the other girls. She is smart, and she knows what she wants to do with her future. I can talk to her about anything, and she understands me. She believed in me when no one else did."

The sheriff listened, and he believed that Anton was being sincere. He felt pity on him, and he didn't want to fight with Anton any longer. He wanted to keep his relationship with his daughter, even if it meant accepting Anton. He stood up, and Anton's heart began to pound.

"If you respect my daughter and respect me, I don't see why you can't see Taylor. But if you do anything to hurt her, you will have to answer to me." Anton smiled. "I want hurt her, sir," he said.

"Well then, you have my blessing."

Chapter 49

TAYLOR PUT ON her new black dress. It was slim to her body and had buttons that ran down her back. She went to the mirror and applied her makeup. She put on her black shoes and thought she would carry her black Coach purse.

She was excited, because this was the first time Anton was going to come to her house to pick her up. She had to cook dinner early and straightened up the kitchen before she left, but she didn't mind. Her father was in the living room watching television, and it seemed that he didn't mind or give it any thought that Anton was coming over.

She had prayed for this moment, and now it was here. Her dream had finally come true. All her life she had wanted to date Anton. Now she was, and it felt like she had imagined it would. She checked herself one last time in the mirror. Everything was perfect. She had bought her dress on Thursday. She and Zoe looked in four dress shops before deciding on the black dress.

It fit her nicely. Her shoes were perfect too. They were not too high or too low. She thought about the time when Anton first asked her out and how much she wanted to be like Ashley and Tammy. Now she laughed at the thought, because Anton liked her for who she was.

She felt a little sad for Ashley and Frank, who were gone to soon. She would have liked to have known Ashley a little better. She only knew her from school, and the only time they really spoke was when they would pass each other in the hall. Maybe she could get to know Tammy a little better.

*****

The doorbell rang, and the sheriff got up to answer it. It was Anton, and he had a bouquet of flowers. The sheriff motioned for him to come in.

"Hi, Sheriff," he said as he came through the door. The sheriff shook his hand.

"What are you doing?" Anton asked.

"Watching the championship game. The Astros are leading two games to one."

"I know. They might make it to the World Series," Anton said with a smile. "I hope so. I've been waiting for this day for a long time," the sheriff said. "Taylor!" the sheriff called.

"I'll be out in a second!" Taylor yelled back.

"She has been getting ready all day, and she's still not ready," the sheriff said laughing.

"Well, you know women." Anton smiled.

Taylor came out of the back, and Anton's heart skipped a beat when he saw how beautiful she looked. He knew she was pretty, but that dress made her look amazing. He walked up to her and handed her the flowers.

Taylor's heart burst when she saw the flowers. The bright colors of reds and yellows were like candy to her eyes. She took the flowers and walked over to the dining room table and set them down.

"I'll put them in a vase for you, Taylor," the sheriff said.

"Thank you," she said as she grabbed her purse. "We won't be late." "Have a good time," the sheriff said as he followed them to the door. The couple stepped outside, and Taylor looked across the street at Mrs. Smith's house and saw her looking out the window. The sheriff waved as Mrs. Smith pulled the curtains closed. Taylor and Anton got into the car, and the sheriff waved as they drove off.

*****

The church was full of young people when Anton and Taylor walked in. Alex was standing with Jonathan and Deputy Jerry when he looked up and saw them.

"There is Anton," Alex said. He went over and shook Anton's hand "You made it," he said.

"Pastor Andrews is over there talking to Deacon Johnson. Do you want to introduce yourselves?" "Yes," Anton said.

Alex led them over to Pastor Andrews. "Pastor," he said, "these are my guests for tonight. You know Taylor, and this is Anton."

"Hello, Son, and welcome," the pastor said. "I'm glad you could attend tonight. Do you belong to a church?"

"No, sir," Anton answered. "I was thinking about joining this one."

"Well amen. Good for you. After service can we talk?" "Yes, sir," Anton said.

"Well make yourself at home."

Anton and Taylor walked over to Jonathan and Alex.

"Services are going to start in a few minutes," Alex said with a smile. Zoe came to the door and looked around. She saw Taylor and walked over to her.

"I'm glad you made it, Zoe," Taylor said.

"I wouldn't miss this for the world," Zoe said. "I had to work today, but I got off early."

Deacon Johnson told everyone to stand up and get out their hymn books. Taylor and Anton took out their books as they sang "Come to Jesus."

The service was nice, and Anton paid close attention to Pastor Andrews's sermon. The pastor had said some of the things that Jerry talked about with him. After the sermon, Anton got up with the other newcomers and joined the church.

Deputy Jerry was proud that Anton had listened to what he'd had to say. After the service, Pastor Andrews talked to Taylor and Anton. He told them that he wanted Anton to join the new members' class before service on Sunday.

Anton agreed and said he would be there next Sunday. When they were finished talking to the pastor, they went over to say goodbye to Alex and Deputy Jerry. Taylor told Jonathan and Alex that she would see them at school on Monday, and then they went out to their car.

Anton looked at Taylor. "You really looked nice today," he said.

"Thank you. you too," she said.

"The service was nice," Anton added.

"Yes," Taylor agreed.

"The sermon was nice too," Anton continued. "Everything was great." Taylor saw that Anton was being a gentleman. It was what she thought all along—Anton was the one she dreamed about. He was the only one who made her happy, and now, after all these years, he was there with her. She knew he would never leave her side. She thanked God for this moment and for answering her prayers. Her heart leaped for joy, and she couldn't believe that her dreams had finally come true.

Anton blushed when he saw how Taylor looked at him. He thought about the time when he wanted to hurt her because of the sheriff, but he wouldn't dare do that now. He was going to hold on to Taylor for as long as he could.

Printed by Libri Plureos GmbH in Hamburg, Germany